Carnal Secrets

HER SUBMISSION

VONNA HARPER

Dedication

To the wild and understanding ladies who share coffee,
gossip, and the occasional discussion of writing with me.
What a tribe we've become!

Books by Vonna Harper

Carnal Secrets

Naked Nights
Her Submission
Taking Her Down

Her Submission

ISBN # 978-1-78686-113-9

©Copyright Vonna Harper 2017

Cover Art by Posh Gosh ©Copyright 2017

Interior text design by Claire Siemaszkiewicz

Totally Bound Publishing

Published in 2017 by Totally Bound Publishing, Newland House, The Point, Weaver Road, Lincoln, LN6 3QN, United Kingdom.

Prologue

"Don't move. Focus your entire being on what's about to happen. Let it become your world. Accept my control."

Eyes tearing, Kaci struggled not to bolt. She'd started shaking the moment Master had unlocked the door to her cell, because last night he'd said today would take her deeper into herself than she'd ever been. Because she knew not to ask for an explanation, she'd spent the night trying to wrap her mind around his words.

"Stand straighter. Show pride in your exquisite body."

Weeks under his control had taught her to obey his every command. Besides, he was right. Despite the whip marks, her body was a thing of beauty. He'd repeatedly told her so and she believed him. Not taking her attention off him, she squared her shoulders. Her arms with the metal cuffs around her wrists remained at her sides. She pressed her legs together until the metal welded to her ankles touched. Her heavy collar forced her to work at keeping her head up.

"Good, slave. To begin, I want you to describe your breasts to me."

Surely he hadn't reminded her of last night's message or brought her out of her cell simply to listen to her repeat words she'd uttered countless times, and yet, she had no choice but to obey. Sometimes he made her apologize for trembling, but this morning his expression made her hope he was simply enjoying his power over her.

"My...my breasts are large for the rest of me. I wear a D cup bra that — "

"What do you wear now?"

"Nothing, Master."

"And why is that?"

"Be-because that's what you want, Master. You want my body always available to you."

The corner of his mouth lifted. "That's right, slave. Go on."

He hadn't touched her today. Most mornings began with a leisurely exploration of her naked body by hands capable of both great tenderness and terrifying cruelty. She never knew which it would be.

"My, ah, my nipples are dark in contrast to the rest of my breasts. The areola – you say my areola are the largest you've ever seen." The longer she returned his gaze, the harder it was to remember what she looked like. Master had crawled into her mind and body and claimed both for his use and amusement. He'd left so little of her that –

"My breasts sag a little, but you tell me I shouldn't be ashamed. Instead, I should take pride in their size and weight. They are gifts to you, yet another part of my body designed for one purpose, to please my Master."

"How do I demonstrate my pleasure, slave?"

His tone had changed slightly, just enough that she knew he was getting ready to take another step in her education. "Many ways." A memory of the last time he'd whipped her breasts compelled her to shake her head in a futile attempt to escape it.

"Be still, slave! What was that about?"

Fear lapped at her. Somehow she kept it from overwhelming her. "I-I'm so sorry, Master. I was thinking..."

"Of your latest lesson in self-control." He reached out and stroked the side of her neck above her collar. "It was perhaps the most intense one I've given you to date."

To date? "I, ah, Master, do you want me to continue?" Her voice wavered and her thigh and calf muscles knotted in preparation for fleeing, but she knew better. Not only couldn't she escape, he'd undoubtedly punish her attempt.

"I don't believe I do. You've demonstrated at least a rudimentary ability to compartmentalize. I ordered you to focus on your breasts and you did. Now, can you guess why I put you through that particular exercise?"

Master was all gray eyes and a body many times stronger than hers. *Determination she now lacked defined him, and he appeared calm in contrast to her constant turmoil.*

"No, Master, I don't know except – you said you'd take me deep into myself today." *Hard as she tried, she couldn't stop from pressing her nails into her palms. She dug her toes at the cement floor.*

He gave her another of his non-smiles. "You remembered. I trusted you would. Stay where you are while I get what I need for this journey."

'No!' she wanted to scream as he walked over to a corner of the room where the table laden with his so-called tools stood. 'You can't expect me to stand here like an animal brought to slaughter!'

But she'd stood and taken her punishment before, because she'd had no choice. Today wouldn't be any different.

Then he held up what he'd selected, and she understood her sanity was about to be tested.

Nipple clamps. Silver. Shining and new. The ultimate contrast to her dark flesh. So large that one filled his palm while the other, attached by a heavy chain, dangled.

Whimpering, she took an involuntary backward step.

"Ah, no," *he said in his overly calm tone.* "Self-mastery, slave. I'm waiting for you to demonstrate the strides you've made in overcoming instinct. Until you've accomplished that to my satisfaction, these lessons will have to continue."

He flexed his wrist so the loose clamp swung back and forth. Fascinated, despite her fear, she studied it. Let it hypnotize her.

Her legs remained planted as he slowly approached. No matter that her breathing had become ragged and she was sweating, she'd do what she must.

"Are you restrained this morning?" *he asked.*

"No, Master."

"Then there's nothing keeping you here? You could leave if you wanted?"

"No, I can't," *she answered, because he wanted that from her.* "The dungeon is locked. You blindfolded me when you brought me to this place, so I don't know where I am. I'm naked and barefoot."

"And ready for restraint, don't forget that."

As if she could. She tore her gaze off the deadly nipple clamp and held up her hands. The thick cuffs gleamed in the overhead light. Next, continuing the ritual he'd beaten into her, she touched her collar. "Ready for restraint, Master."

He smiled. "Just checking your recall. Place your hands behind you and link your fingers together. Regardless of what I do, you are not to alter that position." He changed the swinging clamp's direction so it struck her belly. "If you're unable to comply I'll be forced to handcuff you. You don't want me to do that."

The last time he'd cuffed her had been when she'd failed to mouth-fuck him to his satisfaction. He'd left her restrained like that all night, and in the morning, she'd had no choice but to lap her cold cereal from a bowl on the floor. He'd further demonstrated his displeasure by whipping her as she'd knelt at his feet.

Despite the tremors charging through her, she did as he'd commanded. Having her arms behind her thrust out her breasts. Fear had already tightened her nipples. Now heat bloomed in her pussy in anticipation of what he might do, beyond inflicting pain. Even as she resisted her sexual responsiveness, it would make enduring the unendurable easier. Pleasurable. She licked her lips.

"Pavlov would love you," Master said. "He'd hold you up as proof that a creature can be conditioned to respond to anything."

He was likening her to a dog, but wasn't that what she'd become?

What he'd turned her into?

He gathered up the loose clip. "I haven't used these on you before, because I was waiting for the right occasion. They look like pure silver, but you know my preference for metal. Not only is metal cheaper and more durable, it's heavier."

Heavier.

Swirling emotions closed around her. She all but forgot about her empty stomach and unwashed body. Her pussy remained moist and hot, even though there was no guarantee he'd bring her to climax. Waiting for him to do what he would to her became her world. She understood his intention, knew he'd move at a pace designed to keep her off balance. Each second without pain should be cherished, only she couldn't think beyond how that would end.

Holding a clamp in each hand, he drew his arms apart until the linking chain was stretched tightly. Her breathing intensified and she wondered if she might hyperventilate.

"Good slave." He extended his right hand toward her left breast. "You don't want to flinch because there'll be hell to pay if you do. I was told these don't pinch and that pressure from the springs will keep them in place indefinitely. If they don't perform as advertised, I'll ask for a refund."

One inch became two, followed by more of the deadly approach. She sucked in her belly and started to slink away from him only to stop when he growled. Her mouth wouldn't close and sweat ran down her sides.

"Excellent self-control," he said, "but we both know how difficult maintaining that condition is. The moment this seizes hold of your nipple" – he demonstrated by opening the clamp all the way – "the pain will begin. You've experienced it before, but this is the first time I'm requiring you to bring yourself above the discomfort. To master it instead of surrendering."

He was using his sing-song voice, but much as she tried to absorb it, she couldn't take her attention off the deadly jaws. He was killing her with his slowness, torturing her with anticipation, forcing her to become something beyond herself.

"I need you to do this for me, slave. To prove without a doubt that you understand our relationship and your new role in life." He positioned the gaping clamp over her rigid nipple. "The sooner you do what's necessary, the sooner you'll experience more pleasure than pain. What else? Can you remember what I told you?"

He'd thrown tens of thousands of words at her, and, although she'd tried with everything in her to follow them all, too many were lost within the mess her mind had become. Desperate to put off the horrible moment of ultimate capture as long as possible, she said the first thing she thought of. "You, ah, you want to be proud of me, Master. To be able to show me off to others of your kind. To know they envy our relationship."

A few weeks ago, the way he cocked his head would have made her think she'd pleased him, but she'd learned that the gesture meant she hadn't lived up to his exacting standards. The door to freedom was only a few feet away. If she managed to knock him off his feet, she might escape before he could stop her.

No, she couldn't.

"That's part of it," he acknowledged. Metal warmed by his hand touched her nipple, making her flinch. "But have you forgotten that I derive great pleasure from seeing you suffer?"

No! Please, not that! "I, ah, I haven't forgotten, Master."

"Good, then." His expression softened enough that if she didn't know better she'd believe he was taking pity on her. "I didn't think you would. It's hard keeping track of everything I'm teaching you, I'll grant you that." He sighed. The clamp pressed lightly against her flesh. "My fingers are growing tired. Time for you to do everything you're capable of to please me."

Once again, she fought the desire, the desperate need to beg him not to hurt her, but he'd taught her that such pleas were useless. Swallowing repeatedly and gripping her wrists with all her strength, she waited.

Dread lanced her.

"Straighten, slave. Show pride in your ability to suffer."

From a reservoir deep inside, she found the insane courage to do as he'd ordered. Panting, she stared at him so she wouldn't have to look at his hand. Bit by bit, the pressure against her swollen nipple increased. In a dim and unimportant way, she knew he was drawing out the moment of ultimate capture.

Pressure gave way to pain. Fingers of agony spread over her breast and reached her throat. More discomfort settled in her belly. Undone, she tore her gaze from the man who owned her and stared down at what he'd done to her. The nipple clamp was fastened to her, a potent and powerful monster she didn't dare tear off. Deep, rapid breaths did nothing to lessen the hated sensations. Sobbing, she curled in around herself.

"Good. Let this exquisite tool's mastery spread over you. You can't free yourself from it, can you, slave? If you try, I'll simply restrain you and start over, won't I?"

Speak! Don't beg. "Yes, Master, you will."

He brushed his knuckles over the side of her neck. "Do you want me to do that? Maybe it'd be easier if responsibility for your body is out of your control. You wouldn't have to do anything except endure. No being forced to exhibit self-restraint."

Master loved giving her choices, not that they really were. Regardless of what she said, the outcome would be the same. Pain. Maybe answering him wasn't important. Today was nothing more than something to get through. But once, she'd been a woman who'd made decisions and had been in charge of her life. Despite everything he'd subjected her to, the core of that woman still existed.

She no longer had the pride that went with being able to clothe herself, but facing herself was easier if she believed she wasn't completely broken.

Yet.

"I'll stand here, Master. Not…not try to get away."

"Of course you will, my pet. I wouldn't want to have anything to do with you otherwise."

He'd continued stroking her neck during their short exchange, but she'd known better than to be lulled into believing he'd taken pity on her. Pity wasn't part of his makeup. Still fighting the dread that had become a constant, she stood straight. At his slight frown, she arched her spine and presented her breasts fully to him. She tried not to beg with her eyes but wasn't sure how well she'd succeeded. Besides, he knew what she was thinking, what she was praying for.

He knew everything about her.

"You have incredible breasts, slave." He positioned the clamp over her unencumbered nipple. "I take great pride in them."

How could he say that? Her breasts belonged to her, not him. Or at least they had until he'd captured her. Now she wasn't sure there was still a place where he let off and she began.

Biting, clawing agony, this time. No half-instant in which to ready herself. A sharp whine escaped from behind her clenched teeth, but she managed to remain in place while shaking from the hot, hard discomfort.

"Look down at yourself. See what I've done to you."

Her legs burned and her knees were so weak she wasn't certain they'd continue supporting her. In her mind's eye, she saw herself collapse before him. She wouldn't try to remove the nipple clamps because he'd beat her if she did, but she would wrap her arms around his legs and beg him to free her. She'd become a whipped dog.

"A work of art, slave. A magnificent example of what I've turned you into. Look. See if you don't agree."

Although she was afraid to take her gaze off him – he'd proven his capacity for sudden cruelty enough times – she did as Master commanded. Because the oversized clamps covered them, she could no longer see her nipples. Unnatural weight pulled her breasts down. The exquisite – yes, it was that – chain slid over her breasts, swaying in and out and tugging anew with every move. She couldn't help but admire the contrast between soft female flesh and a well-made instrument of torture.

Harsh restraint. Helplessness. What he wanted her to be. Maybe worthy of reward.

"Turn around."

He knew she didn't want to move, which was exactly why he'd said what he had. Even as she sent the command to her legs, she wondered if he'd ever attached clamps to his own nipples. Did he know what it felt like or did his knowledge come from watching her? Her and other captives who'd come before her.

She tried to rotate away from him, while keeping her upper body as motionless as possible so the chain wouldn't swing any more than it already was, but fear made her clumsy. Her feet tangled, causing her to stumble. She shrieked.

"Ah, sorry," he said from behind her as she tried to blink away hot tears. "It wasn't my intention to have that happen." He rested his hands on her shoulders. "However, there's no one you can blame except yourself."

Her breasts burned so much she could barely concentrate. Much as she wanted to scream at him that every bit of discomfort she'd experienced since he'd taken over her world was his doing, she knew better. His fingers ground into her shoulder blades, preventing her from moving.

"I don't want a clumsy slave. Until or unless you've become

graceful, I have no choice but to keep you to myself. Your every move and every inch of your body reflects on me, your Master. I'm a hard man to please. If you are unable to live up to my standards, I'll have no choice but to sell you."

This was hardly the first time he'd brought up selling her. Part of her embraced anything that would take her from him, but would another Master be any better? At least he spoke to her. Someone else might consider her little more than an animal.

More to the point, Master understood that a slave remained a sexual being. He granted her pleasure.

Sometimes.

"I'm sorry." She couldn't keep a whimper out of her voice. "Master."

He let go of her with his right hand. A heartbeat later he slapped her buttocks. "Almost forgot to call me Master, didn't you?"

His blow had been hard enough to knock her forward, as she was sure he'd intended. Agony streamed through her. She couldn't take her attention off the wildly swaying chain. Suddenly her own fingers were on it. Whimpering, she tried to stop the instrument of torture from moving.

"What are you doing, slave?" His fingers vised her left shoulder as he spun her toward him. He glared at her trembling hand on the metal links. "How dare you – "

An apology was on the tip of her tongue, but before she could begin to beg for forgiveness, anger overtook her. She'd been through so much. Master had condemned her to a life barely worth living.

"You don't own me!" she screamed. Because she couldn't think how to release the pressure without injuring herself, she continued to grip the nipple clamps. "You can't do this!" She indicated her abused breasts. "You have no – "

Growling, he closed a large hand around her throat and propelled her backward. Her back slammed into a wall. Terror threatened to overtake her anger, while every fiber of her being insisted she fight the big, imposing man, but he'd kill her if she so much as scratched him. His hold on her neck tightened.

"Hands over your head, slave."

No! No, please! Her entire body now shook and she could barely see for the tears. Choices? She didn't have any. Not if she wanted to breathe again.

Helpless, she did as he commanded. He continued to squeeze her neck until consciousness faded.

"*I understand your actions, slave. You're an animal and animals are ruled by survival instinct. However, you must find your way past selfishness to total obedience. Otherwise, your existence will be a miserable one. Wouldn't you prefer to be treated like a woman than a beast? To experience incredible climaxes in exchange for putting your Master's needs before your own?*"

She couldn't think, let alone answer. Her arms slid down. Terrified of how he'd react to her disobedience, she tried to lift them, but she was so weak. Her knees threatened to buckle.

Chuckling, he released the pressure on her throat so she could suck in a blessed breath. He let her breathe several more times before again cutting off her air supply. This time, she lasted only a few seconds. Then the world grayed and her arms sagged.

"*Put them back over your head, slave. That's the only thing you have to do.*"

She could! She had to! Otherwise he might kill her.

The gray darkened. Her head threatened to explode. She'd beg now, crawl to him on her belly and kiss his feet, anything to please him.

Once more, he granted her the precious gift of air. As she filled her lungs and stretched her arms as high overhead as possible, she waited for the torture to begin again.

"*I wasn't certain this would turn into another training moment,*" *he said. "I'm pleased it has. And, for the record, I'm relatively satisfied with your self-control. Do you believe you can stay where I put you, slave? If I let you go, you'll remain where I want my property to be?*"

'*Property.*' *Flesh and blood belonging to another human being. She nodded as best she could.*

"*Wise choice, slut.*"

He gave her throat a squeeze then reached over her head and pulled the length of chain he'd gotten down to her wrist. Because he'd restrained her here and this way before, she knew the chain was attached to a wheel. He hooked the chain to her cuff then did the same to her other arm. There was enough slack in the chains that she could stand flat-footed with her elbows slightly bent. Hot pain raged through her still-imprisoned breasts.

Master stepped back and studied her.

"All those years of watching your weight and taking care of yourself, and what did you get for it? A Master whose present goal is to mold you to his needs and desires." He came closer. "I've decided your momentary rebellion is the best thing that could have happened today. It brought our relationship into sharp relief. You tried to modify the discomfort I imposed on you. It didn't work. Now I'll teach you the consequences in ways that wouldn't have been possible if you'd complied with every order."

Another step. He extended a hand, hooked his forefinger around the chain, and drew it toward him.

"I'm sorry, Master," she babbled. "I didn't mean – I won't… please…it won't happen again."

"You can't promise me that any more than I'd promise not to punish you." He tugged sharply.

"Oh, Master, Master, please!" Her feet danced and she couldn't stop her head from thrashing.

"I have no interest in a slave's pleas. You should know that by now."

He drew down on the chain, forcing her to lean over as far as she could. She prayed the clamps would slide off, but they continued to grip. To punish. She was crying openly and promising things that made her hate herself when he let go. Relief poured through her, but it was short-lived because he started the rope swinging again. He left her to suffer through the jerking motions. She realized he'd engaged the wheels on the overhead chains so her arms were being pulled straight. He didn't stop until she was on her toes.

Again, he backed away. This time he folded his arms over his chest as if contemplating something he'd created.

"I wish I was an artist," he said. "I'd like to paint you looking like this. At least I have a camera, don't I?"

Did he expect an answer? Maybe she should say something about all the pictures of her in various restrained poses that covered the walls outside her cage. She hated seeing them and the memories that went with them, but there was so little else to look at.

He went to the cupboard stocked with things she loathed and feared and took out a digital camera.

"I'd tell you to smile, but something tells me you aren't in the mood." He positioned himself to her right and maybe ten feet away, then took pictures. "Besides, a smile would make a lie of what you're feeling. Hold still. We don't want a blurry image, do we?"

Her breasts ached and burned. Her leg muscles were protesting, and her arms felt as if they might dislocate. The day he'd taken her, she'd begged him not to hurt her, but now she knew better than to say a word. He wanted her to suffer. And she would.

Whistling, he slowly moved around her immobilized body. The camera made countless clicking sounds as she resigned herself to being immortalized like this for his perverse pleasure.

That was it. She existed to feed his sadistic nature. Would it ever end and, if it did, would she recognize what she'd become?

"What a sweet, compliant slave. A sexy, sexy woman. Do you miss having clothes? Maybe you've convinced yourself that surely someday I'll give you something to wear so you won't feel quite so vulnerable. If you have, I strongly suggest you stop those thoughts. A slave is naked. End of discussion."

She'd once longed for any scrap of clothing, but, next to the need to be able to lower her arms and an end to the throbbing in her breasts, that was unimportant.

"What do you want, Master? Whatever it is, I'll do it. Take you in my ass, eat you, fuck you —"

"I don't need your permission for those things to happen, slave. Surely you know that." He returned the digital camera to the cupboard and took out something she couldn't see. It could be a whip, a switch, even a cat-o'-nine-tails. Why hadn't she tried to overcome him when she'd had the chance?

Because his strength far outstripped hers. Because he might kill her if she —

"When I introduced the nipple clamps," he said, his voice hypnotic, "my intention was simply to demonstrate my control without destroying you. It was a delicate balance, calling for the utmost concentration on my part. You wouldn't know what was happening or why, which was the point. If you thought about it too much or believed your situation was hopeless, I ran the risk of losing you as a functioning human being. Fortunately for both of us, I'm able to walk that thin line. You might believe I'm dissatisfied with you today, but I'm not."

He'd slowly ended the space between them during his monologue and was now so close she could feel his body heat.

"What you probably interpret as disobedience on your part is simply proof that your instincts are intact. A totally obedient slave, one who doesn't have the will to try to protect herself, is a broken creature. I want you on the edge, to have to constantly battle your instinct for survival."

Was that a compliment? Hard as she tried, she couldn't think for her dread and pain.

"Many Masters, probably the majority of them, would disagree with me. To them, it's all about control and subservience. If their slave blindly obeys their every command and anticipates their every need, they believe they've done their job."

Once again, his knuckles pressed against the side of her neck. Once more, she willed herself not to move.

"I want more than a pussy. I want a mind as well. At least part of one."

She dimly comprehended that he was giving her a glimpse into the rest of her life, but could she accept it? Had she given up that much of herself?

"I'm waiting for a response, slave. Before now, I haven't given you the option of willingly serving me. Do you believe you're capable? Are you enough of a woman?"

He'd never called her a woman. To him she was a slave, an animal, or a slut.

"I don't know, Master."

"Perhaps not. Today I'm going to introduce you to a side of

yourself I suspect you're unaware of. The creature who exists beneath the civilized façade."

Don't, please!

Before she could decide whether she dared speak, he ran his hand between her legs, pushing against her inner thighs. She obediently widened her stance. The sensation in her breasts had settled into a constant throbbing, while her up-stretched arms became more and more uncomfortable. He wouldn't care. He had her where he wanted her. "Pleasure and pain. Ecstasy and agony. Two sides of one coin."

Something cold pressed against her pussy, but even if she wanted to escape, which suddenly she no longer did, she couldn't. "Master?" she whispered.

"That's right, Master." The pressure continued. "I own you in every way there is for one person to own another. Fortunately for you, occasionally I'm compassionate and understanding." He chuckled. "However, as we both know, I'm not known for my consistency, nor would I want to be. It works to my advantage to keep you in a state of uncertainty. As long as you don't know what to expect from me, you'll never get a step ahead of me or even be my equal. I'm in control. Always in control."

He often heaped his brand of logic on her. Despite how crazy it sounded, she tried to make sense of what he was saying. At the same time, she was certain that he said what he did, not in order to educate her, but to keep her off balance. She wasn't sure what point he was trying to make. As long as something rested at her pussy's entrance, she couldn't put her full mind to his words.

"You please me sometimes," he continued. "Enough that occasionally I choose to reward you."

Reward, yes! She knew what that meant.

Panting in anticipation, she thrust her pelvis at him, opening herself to him even more. "Master, I want — you know I try to please you."

He slapped her right breast. "Be quiet! If I want to hear from you, I'll let you know."

Trapped in a fresh pain-storm, she fought to remain silent. She couldn't prevent a whimper from escaping, but then he enjoyed hearing that.

"Settle down." His voice was calm now. "Go deep inside yourself. Anticipate. Prepare."

Her breast still pounded, but she did her best to stay calm. She didn't exist beyond this place. Every aspect of her being revolved around this powerful man.

He leaned into her so their faces were only inches apart. Trembling, she looked up at him as he ran his free hand into her hair. He sometimes talked about shaving it off because it was so messy, but she didn't think he would, because he could easily control her by grabbing it. She wasn't surprised when he tilted her head back, just unnerved because she could no longer see his expression.

"I'm going to use a vibrator on you," he whispered. He pressed himself against her trapped breasts. "The most powerful one in my arsenal."

She all but hung in her restraints as her world closed down even more. Only her captive body remained.

"Dance for me, my pet. Thank me for giving you what you want most."

The vibrator slipped past her sex lips and into her already wet channel. It seemed to be larger around than the last he'd invaded her with. Unlike the other with its rubber tip, this one was all metal. There was nothing soft about it, just a manmade instrument designed to arouse and break her down.

He took his time settling it into her, rotating it back and forth. It went deeper and deeper, spreading her pussy walls until anticipation turned into dread.

"Feel as if you're giving birth to a watermelon?" He chuckled and shoved.

With her head back and immobile, she could barely breathe, let alone try to accommodate the invasion. Her sex was being stretched beyond all reason. If he used it to attack her like the nipple clamps did —

"Master! Ah, please."

"Hey!" He jerked on her hair. "What did I say about keeping your yap shut? You don't want me to gag you, do you?"

She hated being silenced. As long as she had the ability to speak, she held out the slim hope that he'd heed her pleas. "No, Master," she whispered. Another appeal for mercy pushed against her teeth, but she held it in.

"I understand. I truly do. There's no denying that this tool is larger than any man's cock, but your sex is designed to be flexible. The manufacturer assures purchasers that no woman has been injured while using it. Of course" – he chuckled again – "you aren't administering it to yourself. That's my task."

As long as he was talking, hopefully he'd simply hold on to the vibrator, but maybe he'd said all he intended to. She hated being handled as if he owned her body, but what choice did she have?

None.

She tried to relax her muscles and empty her mind, but he was too close and all-consuming. She felt as if she were sinking into him, losing what little remained of herself at the same time. Much as she needed back what she'd lost, she took small comfort in knowing he hadn't injured her. Yes, she bore the whip marks he'd planted on her, but he hadn't broken any bones. He could have suffocated her a few minutes ago. He hadn't, because he wanted her alive.

Alive. Breathing.

Waiting.

After what felt like forever and not long enough, the massive invader started vibrating. It barely hummed, a gentle sensation that made it possible for her to dismiss much of her discomfort.

"I tried this on my cock," he said. "Quite pleasurable at the lower speeds. Then it became a bit much. Don't worry, slave, I'm not going to rob you of the opportunity to determine whether I got my money's worth. For the record, the batteries are new. All right, next gear."

Power jolted her. In seconds she stopped trying to accept and sank into forced pleasure. She hadn't been a particularly sensual woman before Master had captured her, but under what he called his tutelage, her body was becoming more and more receptive to stimulation. These days he could make her juices flow simply by touching her. A few times, even as she acknowledged how *vulnerable it made her, she'd thanked him for his gift. He'd smiled. Smiled and turned her into a horny animal.*

She was there now. A panting, moaning creature drowning in sensation. Whatever gear he'd shifted into was everything her helpless body needed. A climax hovered just out of reach. Pleasure licked at her every cell. She was content to hang here, to float, to sigh and tighten her sex muscles around the potent tool.

"Time to get to work, slave. Dance for me."

Warned by his taunting tone, she held her breath. Instead of an accelerated attack on her pussy, however, the vibrator abruptly quit moving. Her drenched inner walls repeatedly squeezed the tool. Then, to her horror, her body began to settle down. With each passing second, she felt the loss of arousal and growing discomfort. Warned by his all-encompassing presence, she knew not to ask what he intended to do.

Suddenly the tool stormed back to life. This time there was no measured build-up. It went from nothing to everything. Pounded at her. Challenged her to survive.

She climaxed, pleasure and fierce throbbing all mixing together. Continuing. Forcing her up a mountain and holding her there.

"I can't, I can't, oh, God, Master! Master!"

"Dance for me, slave. Who rules you? Who is in control?"

Fire charged through her. She short-circuited. Died and came back to life. Died again.

Something dark and powerful shook her into consciousness, but she was too exhausted to do anything except moan as what had begun as pleasure continued to tear her apart.

"Do you surrender, slave?"

She couldn't answer.

Couldn't think.

Chapter One

"You're lucky you weren't killed. I'm sorry, I shouldn't have said that. You're alive and that's what counts."

"Yes, I'm alive."

Five minutes ago, Kaci Winters had nearly gone about her business without talking to the man with the flat tire, but it wasn't as if they didn't know each other. After all, they'd chatted for a whole half-minute earlier in the day. Noticing he'd had trouble kneeling, she'd decided that offering to help was preferable to replenishing the toilet paper in the men's restroom at Pause Awhile Campground. She'd reminded him of their connection, then had taken the lug wrench from him. Once the nuts had become loose, she'd positioned the jack under the car in preparation for lifting it, but he'd taken over.

She hadn't come out and asked what his mobility problem was, but she had stared. That had probably been why he'd mentioned he'd been in a motorcycle accident. She'd expressed sympathy, but he'd shrugged. She should have dropped what had been none of her business but she'd asked the thirty-something stranger with big hands, broad shoulders, and intense gray eyes about his accident.

"It happened three months ago." He paused while returning her gaze. "Have you ever ridden a motorcycle?"

"A few times, but only as a passenger."

"Boyfriend or husband driving?"

She wasn't surprised by the stranger's attempt to learn something of a personal nature, other than that her favorite ice cream was mint chocolate chip. It came with the territory if you were a decent-looking twenty-three-year-old female and the man asking the question was traveling alone. He wasn't wearing a wedding ring, not that that said anything these days.

Like earlier, his gaze was intense. A little disconcerting. A little exciting.

"The guy and I hadn't known each other that long, so he was kind of a boyfriend," she explained. "The way he handled his bike scared me."

He didn't as much as blink. "Enough so that he became an ex?"

"Pretty much."

She'd gotten to her feet after dealing with the jack but had stayed in close proximity in case the man needed help getting the flat off. Whatever his injuries had been, he hadn't lost upper body strength, as witnessed by the easy way he removed the tire. He'd already gotten out the spare and wasted no time sliding it in place. She liked how he handled himself. There was a smoothness to him, a confidence that made her think he'd emotionally gotten over the accident.

That was something they could talk about—putting the past behind them.

Or she would if she'd been more successful at it.

Earlier in the day, she'd walked up the road a quarter mile to the café and adjacent ice cream parlor that did great business in the summer as vacationers headed into the mountains. She'd made her purchase and had been sitting at a picnic table when a new pickup with a fancy canopy had pulled into the gravel parking area. A man had gotten out, and headed right for where she'd been sitting, leaned against her table, and stretched. He'd obviously been in no hurry. She'd been a little concerned about personal space, but she often was.

After her initial discomfort, she'd felt herself being drawn to him. There was something intriguing about him, a commanding presence. A deepness to his gaze, as if he was looking for something in her.

For a moment, she'd thought he'd found it, but that was

crazy. They were strangers.

He'd asked how much the ice cream cost and whether it was good, which had helped her get past her, what, nervous energy? They'd even engaged in a friendly argument about the best flavors. He'd gone into the parlor and had come out with a double strawberry cone.

"Just what the doctor ordered," he'd told her before slowly getting back into his truck.

All the way back to where she was spending the summer, she'd mulled over the brief connection. He didn't turn her on, but there was something about him she couldn't quite shake, a mysterious aura. A man like that might have a place in her fantasies.

Fortunately, he'd never know what direction her fantasies took.

She'd been surprised and a little suspicious to have him show up at the Pause Awhile Campground where she worked, but his explanation that he'd decided he needed a break from driving and had been taking in the waterfalls off the road between the café and the campground made sense. He'd spotted the Pause Awhile sign just as the driver's side rear tire began to go flat. He'd had no choice but to stop driving so he could deal with it. He certainly hadn't expected to see her.

The longer she watched the man, who hadn't bothered to introduce himself, the more intrigued she became. If his vehicle was any indication, he was better off financially than those who rented RV spaces here. He was traveling by himself and, if she said and did the right things, he might decide to spend the night.

Unless she decided she'd rather sleep alone — which she didn't always want to, because at night her imagination sometimes took her into places she didn't understand. What she labeled sexual fantasies got her hot and bothered, all right. They also left her feeling out of control and confused. Where the hell did they come from?

"The not quite a boyfriend with the motorcycle had

some good qualities," she said, by way of continuing the conversation and putting distance between herself and thoughts she didn't need. "A decent job, for one."

"But?"

"But he was into macho, if you know what I mean."

The stranger held out his hand, prompting her to drop a lug nut into his palm. Their fingers didn't touch but came close enough that she'd acknowledged the potential.

"He wanted you to play the little woman?"

"We didn't live together." *I've only done that once. Never again. Maybe.* "He thought that whatever he was doing or wanted to do took priority. I should kick my agenda aside to accommodate him."

"And you're a liberated woman."

Truth was she wasn't certain what label to put on herself. Messed up, for sure. Thinking she was running out of time in which to decide whether she was interested in more than a casual conversation, she watched as he slipped the rest of the lug nuts in place. After lowering the truck, he picked up the lug wrench in preparation for tightening them even more.

"Let me." She held out her hand. "Whoever does this part needs to kneel, and right now that isn't your strong suit."

He stared at her without speaking for so long that she became acutely aware of the male-female component. He wasn't just looking her over, he was going beneath the surface, searching for something he had no intention of sharing with her. It could have been as simple as an older man trying to decide whether a young thing was interested in him, but she didn't think so. She might have been more concerned if they weren't in a public area.

At length, it occurred to her that he was waiting for her to make good on her offer. She took the tool from him and knelt again. It was pushing ninety this afternoon, which was why she had on shorts. Fortunately, he'd pulled onto the grass-weeds that flanked the campground entrance instead of going clear to the rocky area near the office. Her task took a fair amount of upper body strength, but not her full attention. As a result, she remained aware of his presence. He hadn't invaded her personal space the way he had at the ice cream parlor, but neither did she feel apart from him. He struck her as someone accustomed to being in close proximity with another human being. Maybe a wife? Maybe a sex slave?

Sex slave! Where had the thought come from? Damn it, much more of that nonsense and she'd have to see a shrink, something she vowed she'd never do. She wasn't the most squared away person in the world but she was able to function. What more did she want?

A different past.

Done with her task, she looked over her shoulder at the slightly over-six-foot-tall man. His features were in shadow, which made seeing his expression difficult. Being on her knees like this was more intimidating than she wanted to admit. Disconcerting.

And he knew it.

"It's a good thing I don't charge mechanics' rates," she said as she got to her feet. She tightened her hold on the lug wrench. Forget a one-night stand. He was too — something.

"I appreciate it. So" — he looked around — "are you staying with family or friends?"

"I work here."

"You do?"

She could tell he hadn't expected that, but then most people didn't. "It's a summer job, May through October. I get a place to stay and a not bad salary. Get to meet a lot of different people and occasionally work on my auto repair skills."

His disbelieving expression faded a little, to be replaced by something she didn't understand, but maybe should try to.

"You keep saying 'I'. So it's just you doing, what, being a campground host?"

"It's kind of communal living, only with a constantly

changing cast of characters," she said to let him know she wasn't here alone. "I answered a Craigslist ad. They hired me."

"Hmm. It doesn't look like a first-class operation."

"It isn't. People are only supposed to stay for ten days, but my guess is nearly half of the RVs here belong to people who have nowhere else to live. As long as they pay their rent, the owners don't mind."

His nod made her wonder if he could relate, but he didn't strike her as someone who carried his house on his back. His truck was top of the line, his clothes expensive. His dark hair was on the long side. Her guess was he'd been more interested in getting back on his feet after his accident than haircuts.

"All done," she said, indicating the spare tire. "Now you're free to go."

"Free? Yeah, I am."

Unexpectedly, she couldn't think of anything to say. Shouldn't he want to get back on the road? To her way of thinking, she hadn't given out any signals that she was into a roll in the hay. Maybe she'd entertained the thought at first but no longer.

"So you have limitations on how many hours you should drive in a day?" All right, so it wasn't the most brilliant question she'd ever asked, but hopefully he'd get the hint that it was time for him to move on.

He smiled, one of those grins that didn't reach his eyes and made her think he was doing what he figured was expected. "This is the longest trip I've taken since the accident. Part of it was because I needed a change of scenery."

'Change of scenery.' She could relate to that. Restless. Dissatisfied. Always looking for something.

"Put your feet up the moment you get home and keep going with your physical therapy." What was her problem? One moment she wanted him gone, the next she wanted to learn more about him.

"I'd like to pay you for—"

27

"No. Helping you allowed me to get my good deed over with for the day."

On the tail of another semi-smile, he held out his hand. "Thanks for the help. Your parents raised an independent woman."

Her so-called parents had had nothing to do with how she'd turned out. She might have dropped that on him if not for the way he held her hand. He didn't have it in a death grip, but she'd have to work at getting loose.

Memories of handcuffs and locked doors stirred. Damn it! Would she never get that nightmare time out of her system? Barely holding onto self-control, she pulled back. He held on a second longer then released her.

"It's been interesting," he said. "One more question and then I'll let you go back to work. What are your plans once summer's over? This place closes down, doesn't it?"

"Yes." What did he mean by 'interesting' and what had the overly long handshake been about?

"Maybe you're in college?"

"I've taken a few courses." The way he studied her made the hairs on the back of her neck stand up. The damn man intimidated and intrigued her at the same time. "I'm not worried about paying the bills. Something always comes up."

The corner of his mouth twitched. "What's that saying, something about a rolling stone not gathering any moss? You aren't interested in settling down?"

What do you care? "No. There's nothing wrong with that."

"I didn't say there was, but most young women have a life plan. Specific goals."

How do I begin to do that? "Sounds boring."

He appeared to be mulling over what she'd just said, searching for flaws in her so-called logic. Well, damn it, what she did or didn't do with her life was none of his business. Going it alone was the only thing she knew.

He opened the cab door. "I hope you find what you're looking for."

"What makes you think that's what I'm doing?"

"Because you are."

Chapter Two

The stranger hadn't asked her name and she'd never see him again, so why was she having trouble shaking him off? Kaci wondered as she locked herself in the travel trailer that had been her home since she'd taken the job. Of course, she hadn't asked what his name was, but then, she couldn't remember the last time she'd wanted to get to know someone.

Wanted or dared?

"What the hell's your problem?" she muttered. "Pretending to be more complicated than you are?"

She closed the curtain to the window over the toy-sized sink and sat in the lone recliner, careful not to bump the adjacent so-called dining table. She'd nearly turned down the job offer, but she hadn't because at the time she hadn't had any alternative. Despite what she'd told the man with the flat, she worried about being able to pay the bills, not that she had many.

He'd been right. She needed to think about how she was going to feed herself once the weather turned. Maybe she should have asked if he needed someone to — to what? Hell, she knew less about him than the other way around.

Enough!

Hoping to turn off her mind, she aimed the remote at the small TV. She'd been kept busy checking in two new groups, and was hungry. However, sitting for a few minutes while watching a sitcom was preferable to putting something together for dinner.

The comedy was about a large family with three noisy teenagers, a pair of preschool twins, a mother-in-law who lived in the attic, and various other relatives who kept dropping by. Tonight's episode focused on the oldest girl and some argument she was having with her boyfriend. Most of the parents' suggestions were more crazy than helpful, but even with the irritating laugh track, the family members' love for each other was evident.

Hell. Someone should do a sitcom about a family like hers had been, only there wouldn't be anything funny about that.

She leaned back and closed her eyes. A day full of fresh air and physical activity might have been the best thing that had happened to her today. Instead of opening her imagination to scenes and scenarios that would keep her awake and aroused for hours, she'd actually get some sleep.

Sleep. Oblivion. No thinking. No sexual need pouring through her veins.

Naked. Her hands cupping her breasts. Staring at the red indentations on her nipples. Trying not to acknowledge the metal circling her wrists or her collar's weight.

"What was today's lesson, slave?"

"That — that you can and will do whatever you want to me, Master."

"In part, but there's more to it than that."

"I — Master, I don't know what you want me to say."

"That's because you didn't pay attention. Now I'm going to have to repeat the lesson, starting with reapplying the nipple clamps. Come here."

Whimpering, she scooted on her knees. He hadn't given her permission to release her sore breasts, so she continued to cradle them. She propelled herself forward but couldn't get closer to him. He was sitting but somehow retreating. Teasing and taunting her.

"I'm tired of waiting, slave. You know what happens if you displease me."

She did.

Kaci jerked upright. Disoriented, she stared at the TV where a couple of men ogled a new car. Pieces of the too-familiar dream—she hated calling it a fantasy—clung to her subconscious. Much more of this and she wouldn't be able to separate reality from the crazy-exciting and maybe dangerous places her mind took her. Wouldn't that be a mess? Instead of being locked up because she'd been found guilty of a crime, this time they'd throw away the keys because—

Her tinny-sounding doorbell bleated. Cursing, she got up and covered the five feet separating the recliner from the front door. She reached for the knob then stopped. She might still be half-asleep but she wasn't stupid. "Who is it?"

"Bob. From space thirty-seven. I ain't got no water."

In her befuddled state, she wasn't sure whether space thirty-seven was in the west or the east section. She'd dealt with enough water emergencies to know that most of the time the RV owner hadn't properly hooked his rig up to the campground's system. Well, she'd known this wasn't going to be a nine-to-five job.

"All right. Just a minute."

"My wife wants to take a shower. She's pissed."

Tell someone who cares. "I need to stop by the office for the tools," she said. "Why don't you go back? I'll meet you there."

"Yeah, I better. The old lady's about to tear my head off. Says—"

"Don't worry about it. This'll only take a minute."

The man grumbled something. Wondering if he was cursing her, she opened the door and peeked out. Thanks to the miserable excuse for a bug light overhead, she couldn't see much. One thing she was sure of, her guest wasn't standing there waiting for her. Nervousness took a nibble out of her, but she shrugged it off.

She reached for the key to the office and descended the rickety stairs. Damn it, she'd forgotten to put her shoes back on. Fortunately, her feet were calloused. It would take all her self-control not to bawl Bob out if the problem turned out to be what she suspected.

Grabbing the toolkit with the wrenches in it didn't take long. That done, she headed down the, thankfully, sand path that meandered around the various RV sites. Now that she was wide awake, she remembered she'd rented space thirty-seven today to a middle-aged couple with a yapping dog. The wife hadn't been happy about having to take a space deep in the trees. Well, if they'd wanted a prime location, they should have reserved one, not show up at the last minute.

As she approached the RV in question, she noted that none of the interior lights were on. The first day on the job, she'd discovered the campground lacked decent lighting both overhead and along the paths. She'd asked the owners about it. They'd smiled and explained that this was a wilderness area, not a city street. People wanted to get close to nature so they could stare at the stars. As a result, there were countless dark areas. If a person wasn't careful, he or she could stumble and fall. More to the point, not everyone who stayed here was what she'd call an upstanding citizen. Already, she'd dealt with a number of thefts of such things as lawn furniture and barbecues she blamed on the lack of illumination.

Chiding herself for not having grabbed a flashlight, she pondered calling out for Bob, but, late as it was, those in the nearby RVs might be asleep. Hoping she wouldn't stub one or more of her toes, she put down the tool bag and headed for what she hoped was the front door.

"Ma'am?"

She stopped and turned in the direction the male voice had come from. "Yes?"

Whoever it was didn't respond. Near as she could tell, the man was at the back of the deeply shadowed RV. He was probably looking at the hookups.

"Do you have a flashlight?" she asked. "Sorry, I forgot mine."

"I've got… I think I have…"

He didn't sound particularly elderly, just addled. Taking

each step slowly, she closed in on what she guessed was the side of the RV. She stretched out her hand, touched metal. Mindful of the angry waiting-for-a-shower wife, she didn't speak. As she recalled, a number of closely bunched pine trees were at the back of this space, contributing to the lack of visibility.

"Where are you?" she whispered. "My tools... I'll have to go back—"

A form materialized, startling her. She sensed, more than saw, a human shape. Years of watching her back kicked in. No one was going to defend her, if she needed defending. She was on her own. She turned toward the shape, folded her fingers into a fist.

Then something slammed into her and knocked her backward onto the ground. Her head struck hard earth. A hand clamped over her mouth. A weight settled over her, knees grinding against her forearms and preventing her from lifting them. The man—that much she was certain of—grabbed her hair and turned her head to the side with one hand while still gagging her with the other. The way his body rested on her chest, she couldn't draw a decent breath. Much longer and she'd pass out. Terror lanced her, making it nearly impossible for her to think.

Maybe her attacker knew what she was experiencing, because he let go of her hair and mouth. Before she could get her act together, something wide and sticky pressed against her lips. She tried to shake it off, but he stayed with her, hauling her head off the ground and wrapping the gag around her head. He wasn't content with one wrap. By the time he was done, he'd looped her head a total of three times.

"Step one," he muttered.

Her heart hammered so much she thought it might burst, and when he climbed off her and flipped her onto her belly, she did little more than try to squirm away. He grunted and pulled her arms behind her until her wrists were crisscrossed one over the other.

34

The splintered pieces of her mind came back together, and she bucked, screaming impotently into the gag. Again, he sat on her and held her down, still holding her wrists in place with one large hand. This man knew exactly what he was doing.

"A little risky," he continued in the same low tone, "but I need to feel alive."

She didn't know what he was talking about, didn't want to care, but her survival might depend on learning everything she could about her abductor. She wanted to fight. Every fiber of her being screamed at her to struggle, but he weighed a lot more than she did and all that weight was holding her down. With her arms wrenched behind her, she stood no chance of pulling them loose. She knew, because she kept trying.

He was doing something, moving to the side a little and shifting his weight slightly. She bent her knees in an attempt to slam her heels into his back. She strained but couldn't put enough force behind the effort to make any difference.

His chuckle chilled her.

"Not the smartest thing you've ever done, as you'll find out. Now to prepare you for transport."

No! Oh, God, no!

She was still praying to the god she didn't believe in when she realized he'd been reaching for something to restrain her arms with. The something was thin but strong, maybe plastic strapping. He released her left arm and looped the tie around her right wrist. A tug, and the restraint tightened. Try as she did to keep him from recapturing her left arm, he had no trouble doing so. He again crossed her wrists over each other. All too soon, the cruel plastic held them both in place.

"Go on," he whispered and slid back a little so he straddled her buttocks. "Give getting free a shot."

She struggled to separate her arms, to take back ownership of them, but every time she tugged, the plastic dug into her.

"I have to say, strapping is perfect for this purpose. It's

silent and tucks neatly into almost any pocket. As long as you don't test it, you'll be relatively comfortable. It's a hell of a lot more effective than rope, which I know a great deal about. No give to it."

How do you know about rope? Oh, God, what are you?

He got off her. Even though she couldn't see him, she knew he was getting to his feet, using her buttocks to brace himself against. Suddenly his fingers dug into her and he groaned. His breathing quickened and he cursed.

The man from earlier today. The injured one with the strawberry ice cream cone, flat tire, and strange gray eyes.

"I knew wrestling you to the ground wasn't the best idea, but nothing ventured, nothing gained. I've been out of commission too damn long."

He'd decided to capture her even though he wasn't in the best physical condition? It made no sense — unless he'd been unable to stop himself.

What if he was a murderer, a serial killer?

Powerful hands clamped around her elbows. He pulled her onto her feet. Even with his hold so tight he was bruising her, she struggled to wrench free.

He pulled her close and wrapped an arm around her neck, stopping her desperate fight for freedom. "You won't listen to me at this point," he whispered into her ear. "But I'm going to give you a piece of advice, anyway. If I want a woman, she becomes mine. You won't be getting free."

No, no, no! Don't say that!

His teeth scraped her skin behind her ear and sent cold shivers through her.

"Time to get on the road. I've taken enough chances — chances that have worked to my advantage."

He dragged her around to his side. The moment he started walking, she had no choice but to stumble backward. All too soon she lost her footing. He dragged her behind him as if she weighed no more than a child. Unwanted memories charged through her, bringing with them hard lessons. Like years ago, someone had taken control of her. Fighting her captor was more than useless. She wouldn't win this battle.

A corner of her mind tried to remind her that tonight was far different from when she'd been sixteen, but everything was happening too fast for the message to make an impact. Her heels dragged, first on sand then over pine needles and other debris. Would anyone notice?

Would anyone care if she disappeared?

Her captor paused to shift his hold. She tried to dig her feet into the ground. If she'd bothered with shoes, she could have at least left one behind as a clue. Maybe — please let it happen — he'd forget about the tools she'd set down. Come morning someone would see them.

And what?

His too-strong forearm pressed against her breasts while his fingers dug into her armpit. She felt like a small child being yanked around by an angry parent, only it wasn't that simple.

Where was he taking her?

Before long, his breathing became labored and his sweat stuck their clothes together, but he didn't slow down. She'd been handcuffed enough times that she'd believed she understood what being restrained was like. However, either the position he'd placed her in was even more restrictive than anything she'd experienced or fear was adding to her sense of helplessness. He was staying as far from the RVs as possible, and, despite herself, she admired his ability to find his way in the dark. It dawned on her that he must have taken this route before — while planning her abduction.

Doubtless, his intention was to rape her. Maybe he thought he could hold her for ransom, but no one cared enough about her to pay for her return.

Why had she lived her life the way she had, keeping distance between herself and the rest of the world?

"Damn," he wheezed. "I've never been this out of shape."

What was he talking about? Surely he didn't mean he'd done something like this before.

Or had he?

Sick of the never-ending questions she feared she might never have the answers to, she redoubled her efforts to get her feet under her. He stopped and turned her so they faced each other. Beyond him was the dimly lit back lot where, over the years, people had left broken-down vehicles. To her horror, she recognized Ice Cream Man's truck and canopy among the junk.

Please! Someone see me before —

"I'm a hunter," he whispered. His fingers clenched her upper arms. She couldn't move. "What I've learned is that people aren't observant about their surroundings. They see what they believe they're going to see. They don't have survival instincts. You're a classic example."

That's not true! I'd be dead if I wasn't a survivor. Despite her silent argument, she knew he was right. She'd been so stupid!

"Almost there. As I'm sure you've figured out, I don't intend to stay here any longer than absolutely necessary."

The instant he released her left arm, she spun away from him. Before she could escape, he grabbed a fistful of her unruly shoulder-length hair and yanked her head down so she was deeply bent over and looking at the ground.

"You have many of the attributes I was hunting for." His whisper had a seductive quality. Either that or she couldn't think beyond his all-consuming presence. "Including an easy way of controlling you. More importantly, I know what you're like under the surface. Your — I nearly called it a weakness, but it isn't. Your submissive nature is what will make you valuable to me." He tugged down so she was in danger of falling forward. "Let's get this part over with."

He began walking again. Her scalp burned as he forced her to plod, hunched over, after him. An animal being led to slaughter, that's what she'd become.

Or worse.

Please don't do this! I don't deserve…you don't want to do this. I'm a human being, a woman. I don't…I can't…

Lost in wordless pleas, she paid scant attention to where they were going. Gravel dug into her feet.

Then, once again, he stopped. Still using his hold on her hair, he shoved her forward. Her belly slammed into what she guessed was an open tailgate. He let go of her hair. She started to lift her head, but, before she could complete the movement, he grabbed her around the waist from behind and lifted her off her feet, shoving her over the tailgate and into deep darkness.

Cursing, he crawled after her and planted both hands on her buttocks, preventing her from getting off her belly. The smell of rubber nearly made her vomit.

His truck bed. His domain.

Screaming into the gag, she fought like a wild thing. She tried to rock from side to side. That didn't work so she struggled to bend her legs. If she made enough noise —

"Fuck! I know what you're thinking. That problem with that logic is we're playing my game, not yours. The rules are *all* mine."

She continued to battle his attempts to hold her down. He cursed her, which propelled her to redouble her efforts. Unless he'd lied earlier about having been in an accident, maybe she could hurt him enough to disable him. Sobbing, she lifted her upper body off the truck bed and turned her head toward him. Only a faint amount of light reached the truck's interior. As a result, she found herself looking at a great, dark, faceless male form. Much of his weight pressed against her buttocks. No wonder she couldn't get out from under him.

"Just giving you a sample of what you're in for. For the record, the journey has begun."

That said, he climbed on top of her, positioning himself so he faced her legs. His crotch settled over the small of her back. Her lower body was relatively free, but he'd pinned her upper half to the truck bed. She sensed him reaching out and guessed he was drawing something toward him. Grunting, he pushed her shorts down a little and slid his hands, and whatever he'd gotten hold of, under her waist.

Something thick and stiff pressed on her belly. At first, she thought it was a belt, then realized it was a length of leather. Once he had it around her waist, he cinched it so tightly her ability to draw a deep breath was compromised. He grabbed something on the leather at the small of her back and pulled up. It took her too long to comprehend that he must have taken hold of a ring embedded into the belt.

Again, he reached out for whatever he'd placed in the truck bed for his sick use. She kept trying to kick him until he grabbed her left ankle and wrenched her leg up. Rope circled her ankle, tightened. He looped the rope around her ankle several times then slipped what she surmised was the rope end through the ring. In her mind's eye, she too clearly saw him knotting it.

"Half of a hog-tie. Little doggy on the ground in record time for this cowboy."

Despite her dread of what she'd discover, she tried to straighten her leg. He was right. He'd turned it into a useless appendage. She was so sure he'd do the same to her other leg that she was unprepared when he climbed off her. She heard him rummaging around and tried to roll onto her side. Before she could complete the task, however, he returned to her, grabbed her hair, and dragged her toward him so her face was smashed on his thigh. If she could've, she'd have bitten him.

He let go of her hair and placed something around her neck. A fresh wave of terror surged through her. She fought with every bit of strength she possessed, but it wasn't enough. The something tightened. A snapping sound left her with no doubt that he'd hooked the ends together.

A collar. Made of leather. Not as thick or stiff as what circled her waist, but equally horrifying.

"It keeps getting worse for you, doesn't it?" He patted her cheek. "For the record, I'm nearly done for now. The only thing left to do is making sure you stay in place."

I'm dead. He's going to kill me.

She barely noticed what he was doing as he slid the collar around her neck. He slapped her cheek. Brought back into the moment, she whimpered.

"Just making sure you're still with me. Sometimes captives check out, but I won't let you do that. The more aware you are, the more complete the lessons. Like I said, time for us to get underway."

He hooked his finger through what had to be a ring in her collar and pulled her closer to where the truck bed and cab joined. An ominous clicking sound at her throat told her what she didn't want to know — that he'd chained her to the vehicle. She could turn her head from side to side, but the truck had become her prison.

Not again! Not the past coming back to life.

She'd been shaking since the nightmare had begun and was close to losing bladder control. What she'd been through as a teenager hadn't prepared her for this. Nothing could have.

Masculine hands massaged the backs of her shoulders. Dreading what he'd do next, she held her breath. From time to time, her old man had owned what he called guard dogs. Instead of letting them run loose so they could keep an eye on what passed for the family's property, he'd kept them chained to dog houses. That's what she'd become, her captor's pet.

Pet?

Worse than that.

After massaging her for several seconds, he left her. The moment she realized he'd climbed out of the truck, she scooted back, desperate to learn how much freedom he'd left her with. She'd gone only a few inches before the collar tightened. Sobbing wordlessly, she pushed herself forward to take the pressure off her neck. After a while she tried to roll onto her side, but her deeply bent elbows stopped her. She next tried to slam her free leg against the floor in an attempt to draw attention to her but couldn't put any strength behind the effort.

Sick at heart, she lay still. He had her.

Could and would do whatever he wanted to her.

Reality was different, far different from her naïve fantasies.

Chapter Three

Pulling off the capture called for skills Reno had honed over years of doing a job only a few were capable of. He knew what had to be done without needing to think about the steps. So why was he taking so damn long tonight?

The answer came as he headed for the trailer where the subject had left her tools. He wasn't at the top of his game. No matter how much he wished it wasn't so, he hadn't fully recovered from the motorcycle accident that had nearly killed him. As he'd been actively engaged in securing her, he'd managed to ignore his left leg. Now the deep ache reminded him that he'd nearly lost it. It would never be the same. Managing pain and compromised mobility took a lot out of a man.

A sex slave trainer.

At least the accident hadn't compromised his vision. He could still see better than most people, particularly at night. Teeth clenched against the throbbing crawling through his thigh muscles, he hurried to the trailer with the probably still sleeping couple and picked up the tool bag. It was heavy enough that he admired the subject's ability to carry it the way she had.

The veins in his temple pulsed, forcing him to stop and wait for his blood pressure to back off. His hearing was as acute as his eyesight, enabling him to catch the reassuring snores from inside the metal can. Having this particular RV, with those particular owners, in this remote space had made the capture possible. That, and the lack of security lighting. If not for those fortuitous elements, he'd probably be nearing home while trying to shake off the memory of the one who'd gotten away.

She hadn't.

She was his.

To do what with?

The unexpected question stopped him halfway to the office, where he intended to leave the tool bag. Damn it, he was like a dog that had been chasing sticks all his life. He shouldn't be asking himself why he was still chasing them.

Teeth clenched, he silenced the mental questions. He was damn good at what he did, and tonight was a prime example of his skills. He was back in the saddle, so to speak. He'd been watching her so he knew where she'd gotten the bag from. It hadn't occurred her to lock the office door, which made putting it back in place easy. He pulled a cloth from his back pocket and wiped off both the bag and doorknob. He debated locking the door but decided it didn't make any difference.

At the beginning of his career, he'd been eager to spend as much time with a subject as possible, but the years of work and too-long hospitalization had taught him patience. He'd take a few minutes to look through the shoebox-sized trailer where she lived. She'd keep.

Once he was in it, he took advantage of the light from the TV to check out his surroundings. He grabbed her cell phone and the small back pack she used as a purse. Leaving her car behind might arouse someone's suspicions, but maybe not if he took most of her clothes. That way, people might conclude she'd taken off with some man with a vehicle that was in better shape than her beater.

She had taken off, just not willingly.

It surprised him to discover she didn't have a laptop. He could check her cell phone for information about family and friends. Unless, he learned different, he'd assume she wasn't hooked into social networks.

Was a loner.

Sometimes the stars aligned perfectly.

Like now, when he needed to feel alive.

* * * *

No surprise, the subject was where he'd left her. If he were doing this by the book, he would have truly hog-tied her so there was no way she could make enough noise to alert someone to what had happened to her, but tonight was about living dangerously. Remembering what had given his life purpose before a sharp turn and water on the pavement had—

Not going there!

He tossed her belongings near her then closed the canopy door and got in the cab. His bad leg screamed at having to briefly support his weight, but at least his right was in shape for handling the gas and brake pedals.

Likening himself to a hunter who'd just bagged a trophy kill, he started the engine and put the truck into drive. He felt disloyal to the rig for briefly leaving it in this sad metal graveyard, but anonymity was the name of the game. On the off chance that someone wrote down the license plate number and reported it to the police, the cops would discover it had been taken off a twenty-year-old sedan.

After putting some ten miles between himself and the campground, he pulled over and stopped so he could examine his captive's cell phone. To his surprise, there were only two numbers in her address book. The only saved message was nearly three weeks old and consisted of a short comment about how well she'd handled a space renter's bounced check. He concluded that her boss had left the message. That number was one of the two in her address book. The other had an out-of-state area code.

Both satisfied that hordes of friends wouldn't be searching for her, and feeling unexpected sympathy since she was so isolated, he wiped off the cell and chucked it out of the window. He took a moment to massage his leg then got on the road again.

* * * *

Reno put a good fifty miles between him and the capture site before he looked for a place to stop. It was after midnight and he was deep in the mountains, but, more to the point, he hadn't encountered another vehicle for at least fifteen minutes. He didn't often take this route between his cabin and his closest work site since it was the slow way, but he'd been in no hurry. In fact, for the first time since he'd built the cabin, he hadn't been eager to return.

As he recalled, there were a couple of gravel roads in this area that led to fishing lakes. Fishing had never interested him, but he didn't intend to go to the lakes, anyway. He'd spotted a wooden sign pointing to the right and took the pitted single-lane road, driving as slowly as possible because the ruts made the truck bounce, jarring his still-repairing body. Too bad he couldn't see the subject being tossed about. He'd have to check to make sure she wasn't getting choked.

A little uneasy at being in unfamiliar territory, he nosed the truck as far off the road as possible and put it in park. He'd been driving with the windows down and the heater on. As a result, cool air almost immediately enveloped him. The smell of pine, pitch, and dirt brought back peaceful memories of the place he called home, and he relaxed.

Damn, but he loved the log structure. The explanation for his reluctance to return home was simple—he had cabin fever—that, and memories of how hard getting around had been since checking himself out of the hospital against doctors' orders.

Experience had taught him how long a subject could be kept in one position without risking damage to the merchandise, and this one was getting close to that limit. Much as he wanted to lean back his head and sleep, he didn't dare.

At least as near as he could tell, today's unexpected exertion hadn't set him back physically. He could live with aches and pains, they were nothing new.

Feeling more upbeat than he remembered feeling in too

long, he walked around to the back and opened the camper door. He couldn't see, but his well-honed senses left him with no doubt that his captive was where she was supposed to be. Her quick breaths reinforced what he already knew. He'd left enough slack in the chain hooking her collar to the truck so that, as long as she didn't lose her mind, she'd be able to breathe normally. Of course, the position was far from comfortable, but that was the point, wasn't it?

Breaking them down slowly.

For a reason he wasn't interested in exploring, his upbeat mood faded. The question of why he was doing this tried to break free, but he shoved it aside. He crawled in with her and felt his way to her head. From the moment he'd spotted her at the ice cream parlor, he'd realized she was in decent physical condition. Wrestling her into submission had added to his admiration of her body. Now he expanded his knowledge by running his fingers under her sleeveless T-shirt at the waist and inching up her back. He'd taken care to make sure her clothes were out of the way before putting on the waist restraint, but deliberately hadn't touched her upper body. Some of his fellow Carnal Incorporated employees went at controlling a subject as if they were branding a calf. He had his own tried and true way, which called for the slow approach. Messing with their minds before turning to their bodies.

Keeping himself in check wasn't easy. He hadn't fucked since shortly before his accident. For the first month, sex hadn't been on his radar, but then his dependence on painkillers had decreased, and his body was reminding him that he was accustomed to having sex as often as he wanted. The opportunity hadn't presented itself for a long time and he'd made do with jerking off.

Women's forms were amazing things. Despite how many he'd handled, and there'd been a lot, they still turned him on. He loved their soft flesh, quivering muscles, hard bone. The sound of one in distress spoke directly to his cock, which he took as proof that he'd chosen the right career — or it had chosen him.

This one smelled of sweat and fear. To her credit she hadn't lost bladder control—yet. Thinking of her need to pee reminded him of the same need, but he continued to stroke her back. The top was trapped under her, and he couldn't reach all the way to her shoulders, but he was still aware of her straining muscles. He trusted his instincts and experience so hadn't given much thought to how he'd restrain her. Once he'd realized how flexible she was, he'd hit upon placing one wrist over the other behind her back. The position forced her breasts out. He wasn't ready to start exploring them, but it didn't hurt to give her a taste of what she was going to experience.

Fighting the horny beast just below the surface, he raked both sides of her spine as thoroughly as he could with her arms in the way. She shuddered and whined into the gag. He debated marking her backbone, then decided to make her wait. Make both of them wait.

Reminded of the need for self-restraint, he stopped his pleasurable task and reached for where the neck chain was fastened to the truck and unhooked it. Wishing he could see what he was doing and what she looked like, he pulled her toward him.

"This is your leash." He shook the chain. "The way I'm going to keep you under control. I know I'm pointing out the obvious, but I believe in letting a subject know some of what's happening to her."

Not a subject, but a sex slave, something you'll figure out in time.

He reeled in some more until her head rested on his good thigh. She strained to put distance between them, but he had no trouble keeping her where he wanted her. He patted her cheek.

"I trust you're trainable. In fact, I'm damn sure of it. Call it one of the benefits of being in my particular business for as long as I have. Believe me, you aren't going to like it if you don't go along with the program." He chuckled and patted her cheek some more. "Come to think of it, there's probably only one thing you're going to like about what will take place for the foreseeable future."

A muffled protest from her gagged mouth distracted him from what else he'd been going to say. He reminded himself not to hand her too much information, then slid the chain under his knee, which freed both of his hands. Her head still rested on his thigh, only he had no doubt *she* wouldn't use the word rest.

It was unimportant. He had work to do.

Because he always used a square knot, he easily untied the leg rope from her waist restraint. She sobbed as he straightened her leg. He waited for her breathing to settle down then tugged on the rope to remind her that it was still around her ankle.

"We're going outside," he informed her. "Just you and me and the woodland creatures. We're going to pee and then I'll decide my next move. For your information, we're in a national forest. Even if you still had your cell phone — I got rid of it — you probably couldn't get reception here."

Going by feel, he took hold of her elbows and levered her into a sitting position. Come morning he was going to take a long and lustful look at his latest acquisition, the creature he hadn't known he was going to grab until he'd seen her.

"This can go one of two ways. Either I haul you out of here like some misbehaving dog, or you take the initiative and get out on your own. Which is it going to be?"

She mumbled something. Even with all his experience dealing with gagged subjects, he couldn't make sense of what she was saying.

"Make up your damn mind," he grumbled. With every second, he was becoming more tired, proof of how much energy he'd expended today and how little he had in reserve.

By way of response, she sagged forward. He wasn't naïve enough to believe she'd surrendered. More likely this was momentary weakness on her part. Sooner or later, they'd have the battle royal. He was looking forward to it.

Hell, he'd embrace anything that took him out of himself.

"I'm not taking your word for it." He chuckled. "Here's how it's going to play out. Slide forward until you reach the end of the tailgate. Once you're there, I'll help you stand. One wrong move on your part" — he jerked on the chain — "and you'll regret it. Understand?"

After a telling moment she nodded.

Instead of ordering her to get moving, he waited to see what she'd do. He sensed more than saw her scoot forward on her buttocks. Twice, she lost her balance and fell onto her side. He got out. As soon as she'd righted herself, he encouraged her to get going again via the handy chain.

Well-versed in the power of silence, he gave her no warning before taking hold of her belt in front and yanking her the last few inches. She started to tip forward so he wrapped his arms around her and guided her legs to the ground.

The Carnal manual called for pushing her away as if he wanted nothing to do with being near her. Despite that, he kept her close as her young warmth spread through him. He hadn't held a woman for so long. More to the point, he couldn't remember the last time one had willingly embraced him.

Get over yourself! You made your bed and know how to lie in it.

Despite his self-anger, he couldn't help but wonder if she, too, had needed the contact. For just a second, she'd gone all soft and loose.

He'd left the headlights on since his intention had been to walk them into the woods before doing their business, but her being barefoot made him reconsider. Even if his body was up to it, he wasn't about to carry her.

Dismissing her grunts of pain caused by whatever she was stepping on, he brought her around to the front of the truck and pointed at the ground. "There's your bathroom — unless you want to keep on walking."

Her head went up and she stared at him with huge

shocked eyes. Then she looked at the woods and shook her head.

"I like a woman who can make decisions. Here, I'll help you."

Hopefully before she could figure out what he had in mind, he unzipped her shorts and pulled them and her underpants down to her ankles. Her already ragged breathing became more labored, and she turned her head away from him. Before he needed to swat her ass in encouragement, she opened her legs as far as she could, thrust her pelvis backward, and squatted. He had to admire her balance. As far as he could tell, she managed to keep urine off her clothes. When, head still averted, she straightened, he pulled her practical panties and well-worn shorts back into place but didn't bother with the zipper.

Holding tightly to the chain, he extracted his cock and covered her urine with his. He wondered if she got the point, which was that he was marking his territory.

Determined to continue the lesson, he roughly pulled her back to the truck bed and hoisted her into it via a firmer than necessary hold on her midriff. As she struggled to a sitting position, he painfully climbed in next to her. Darn it, if he hadn't disabled the canopy's light he'd be able to study her expression and give her a clear view of what her prison looked like. Again, going by feel, he refastened the neck chain to the bed wall at her back. Her arms had been behind her for longer than was good for them, but he didn't want to take any risks until he was sure she was well restrained.

He had to reach around a little before he· found the rope attached to her one ankle, then fumbled a bit more until he located another of the metal fasteners welded to the bed's side. He threaded the rope through it, tugged it tightly, and knotted it. She still had one free leg, but it was on the side opposite from where he crouched.

After shortening the chain so she was off balance and in danger of falling backward, he withdrew his knife from his pocket and cut through the plastic ties around her wrists.

He prepared himself for a battle, but she didn't resist as he pulled her arms in front, positioned the belt so the ring was near her navel, and, using another length of rope, tethered her wrists to the ring.

Rocking back on his heels, he kneaded her shoulders and upper arms. "I'm not a complete bastard. In fact, by the time I'm done with you, you're—I was going to say you're going to worship me, but that's getting ahead of the game. Here's the deal. We're going to stay here for a few hours while I get some sleep. There doesn't appear to be anyone around for miles so I'm going to take a chance on ungagging you. One unapproved word out of you and you'll regret it, got it?" He dug his fingers into the hollow above her collarbone.

She tried to wrench free. However, all she accomplished was to tip backward until the truck wall stopped her. He left her half sprawled as he unwound the tape by feel. Her hair stuck to it in a million places but finally he got it off.

He placed his hand over her mouth. "Remember what I said, no trying to call for help."

Her slow nod said two things. One, he could believe her. Two, right now she hated more than feared him. Wondering why her opinion of him mattered, he stroked her lips. She shuddered but didn't try to bite him.

"Good response," he told her. "If you continue to have a measure of self-control, you'll get through this."

"What…what are you going to do to me?" she whispered.

"That's for me to know and you to find out."

"Why? I haven't done anything to—"

"Why? You're a lovely young thing and I make my living off women like you."

"No! You can't—"

"Yes, I can." He slid his hands down her arms to her wrists, making his point. "I have and I will. End of discussion. Like I said, I need some sleep." He worked his fingers back up her arms. Then, because every moment with a subject should be part of a greater lesson, he cupped his hands around her breasts. Even with her top and bra in the way, he acknowledged her hard nipples. Several things could cause a woman's nipples to harden, fear and arousal primary among them. If arousal factored in, that reinforced what he'd sensed about her during their brief discussion of ice cream.

"Mine," he told her. "From now on, these belong to me."

Chapter Four

Kaci felt as if she were falling deeper and deeper into a dark hole. She repeatedly tried to empty her mind so she could get the rest her body desperately needed, but she couldn't. The man had loosened the awful chain attached to the collar enough that she'd been able to lie down. Her arms didn't hurt as much as they had when they'd been behind her, but she hated how useless they were. The ankle tie was overkill. Without use of her hands she couldn't possibly unhook herself. He'd thrown most of her clothes into the cab-over, which meant, what, that he intended to keep her with him indefinitely?

Trapped. Caught. Deep in the mountains she loved. Lost.

The man who'd done this to her—she didn't want to know his name—had rolled out a sleeping bag and pillow and was stretched out near her. Of course, her comfort didn't matter to him. Maybe he didn't care whether she lived to see tomorrow.

At least he hadn't stripped her naked, she repeatedly told herself as cold night air made her shiver even more. Her shorts were still unzipped, but at least they were back in place.

He'd touched her breasts.

Damn it, she'd known that sooner or later he'd do what he had so why was the act itself so hard to accept?

Because there wasn't a thing she could do to stop him.

Tears threatened to break loose. Furious and scared, she fought them. Never, never again would she let anyone, especially herself, see her as weak. If she was going to die, she'd die strong.

She tried to turn onto her side, but, between the damnable chain and her bent elbows, she couldn't. For the hundredth time, she tested the security of the rope around her wrists. The way he'd tied them reminded her of pictures she'd seen of people wearing straitjackets.

If he'd done that on purpose—

He knew what he was doing. Oh, God, he'd singled her out, set his sights on her, watched her, planned her capture.

And now that he had her—

Where was he taking her?

Why?

Not for the first time, she chided herself for the stupid question. He intended to hold and repeatedly rape her. A tear leaked out from under her closed right eye. Just last night she'd mentally created a vivid fictional scenario of what her life as some all-powerful Master's sex slave would be like. She'd controlled every move and word both of them said and the rich scenes had turned her on, as they always did.

What a fool she'd been. Reality was nothing like her sexual fantasies.

* * * *

Kaci jerked awake. She guessed she'd only been asleep for a few minutes, but during that time her mind had both cleared out and filled with the thoughts she'd been resisting since the moment he'd taken her. Eyes open and staring at nothing, she forced herself to stay with them.

For years, she'd nurtured fantasy visions of herself as a sex slave. She'd chalked her deeply personal obsession up to a number of things, including her sadly limited sex life. By the light of day, she resisted acknowledging how much the real-as-life scenarios aroused her, but she couldn't deny that she found them exciting—and far different from how she lived her life.

Years ago, the legal system had controlled her every

minute, and she'd hated it. Once that awful time was over, she'd vowed to become her own woman, to call the shots and make her own decisions.

During the day, she took pride in being able to live by that standard. Nights, however, were different. Something she let run wild.

Just letting off a little emotional steam, she repeatedly told herself. Mentally playing with the absolute opposite of free will as a way of dealing with her past.

The question that had been waiting to break free continued to push at her. Fighting it, she squeezed her eyes shut, but that didn't help, and after a brief battle she gave in.

What if her captor had somehow seen into her?

What if he knew about where her fantasies took her?

Planned to use them to his advantage?

* * * *

Every muscle in Kaci's body ached, and her head hurt from the lack of sleep. She was hungry.

By her reckoning, which she didn't fully trust, her captor and she had been back on the move for a couple of hours. He'd woken as it had been getting light and had taken her out so she could pee again. At first she'd been determined not to say anything to this creature who treated her like a dog, but her dry mouth had gotten the best of her.

"I'm thirsty," she'd said.

"If you want me to do anything about it," he'd replied, "you're going to have to ask."

"Please." Saying the word had nearly made her gag. "I'd like a drink."

It hadn't been enough. He'd wanted more from her, to take her deeper into submission. Knowing he could and would hold out much longer than she could, she'd begged. Opening her mouth while he'd held a water bottle to her lips had been horribly demeaning and yet she'd survived. She'd even thanked him without needing to be prompted.

They'd been on a gravel road for several minutes now, and the damn man was making no attempt to dodge potholes. As a result, she kept bouncing. Her buttocks might be bruised, her back ached from trying to remain in a sitting position, and her tethered leg had cramped. At least, she reluctantly reminded herself, she was no longer thirsty.

Would he give her something to eat?

Maybe he intended to let her starve. Once she was weak enough, he'd exploit her weakness to force her to demean herself even more than she already had.

The canopy had narrow windows on both sides, and she could see evergreens. Shortly after getting underway this morning, the truck had started going downhill. She'd hoped that meant they were leaving the mountains and coming to a more populated area, but then they'd started climbing again. She'd tried to orient herself but hadn't been able to. They might not even be in the same state as yesterday.

Disappeared.

Gone.

No one who'd care what happened to her.

On the verge of again feeling sorry for herself, she recalled that she'd chosen this solitary life. One good thing — if her captor's intention was to hold her for ransom, he was out of luck. Maybe he'd get tired of having to keep an eye on her and let her go.

No, he wouldn't.

The truck slowed, made a sharp left-hand turn and continued. She wanted it to speed up so they'd come to the end of this nightmare journey. Unfortunately, it crawled and bounced, the surrounding trees closing around her. So, this was what driving into Hell was like.

Finally, they stopped moving. The engine went silent. Blind fear assaulted her, compelling her to thrash about. All she accomplished was to fall over, striking her elbow as she did. She wound up on her stomach, her trapped leg twisted under her, the chain against her cheek, and her weight resting on her arms. Her heart hammered. Maybe she was having a heart attack.

She heard the driver's door open, closely followed by the sound of shoes crunching on gravel. Much as she hated letting her captor see her like this, she had no choice. One minute passed followed by another. She strained, listening for a sound from him, but heard only pine needles being shaken by the wind.

At length, she tried to push herself back around but couldn't with her fingers against her body, or rather they were against the horrible leather restriction around her waist.

Time passed. The wind whispered, and at another time the sound would have comforted her. Instead, she tried to imagine what he was doing. He'd gone inside whatever place he'd taken her to and was in no hurry to return for her. Did he live alone? If not, was it possible that whoever he shared his home with would insist he let her go?

Unless that person was the same devil's spawn.

I don't deserve this! After what I went through growing up – please, I just want to be left alone!

Her thoughts looped and looped. She couldn't find a way out of them. Her captor had brought her here to torture and rape her. In essence, she'd dropped off the face of the earth. Her boss would conclude that she'd walked out on the job, maybe because she'd taken off with some man with a better car than her beater. Years from now someone would find her bones.

Self-pity had never been her style, but it became part of the mess in her mind. For the first time in her memory she wanted her parents.

* * * *

Kaci's legs nearly went out from under her, but not just because she'd been restrained for so long. Minutes ago, saying nothing about the condition he'd found her in, her captor had untangled her and hauled her out of his truck.

The rope around her ankle trailed behind. She figured he'd left her for the better part of an hour. In sharp contrast to her stinking body, he smelled of soap and shampoo and had obviously just shaved. It wouldn't have surprised her if he'd eaten first, but maybe he'd simply wanted to enjoy his place before soiling it with her presence.

Given all the evergreens she'd seen earlier, she guessed he'd brought her to some isolated cabin, but she could hardly call the magnificent structure that. She'd concluded that there weren't any neighbors. He had this incredible place to himself.

A great stone chimney dominated the two-story building's left side. The other walls were finished with what she guessed were cedar shakes. At first glance, she'd thought the roof was made from wood shingles. Then she realized it was a manmade product, probably as defense against fire danger. The large, multi-paned windows were framed in red, which made them stand out.

An expansive porch, braced by logs, sheltered the front door. Two-foot high stonework that marched around the entire structure had probably been designed to mask the foundation. She guessed the cabin had to be at least two thousand square feet.

"Yours?" she finally got out. "You live—"

"Yeah, it's mine."

She knew pride when she heard it, which was understandable. A handful of times she'd allowed herself to conjure up what her dream home would look like, but her imagination hadn't been vivid enough to come up with something this beautiful. A red cinder footpath led from where he'd parked the truck to the front door. Other than that, nature was in charge of the landscaping. Wild grasses covered the open areas and towering pines flanked the house.

"I wanted you to see this before—" He tightened his hold on the chain and lifted it, forcing her onto her toes. "Before we go inside."

He wanted her to be in awe of what belonged to him, and she was. No way could she hide her reaction from him.

"Wait," she begged and dug her toes into the cinder. "At least tell me if there's someone inside."

"No."

If he'd answered one question maybe she could ask another, but did she want to know what he intended to do to her?

"I know what you're thinking," he told her and began leading her toward the ominous-looking log front door. "You're convinced I'm an insane beast and you're going to be killed, but that's the last thing I'd do. You're too — valuable, alive."

She couldn't wrap her mind around what he'd just said. Maybe some of her incomprehension came from being lightheaded from hunger and fear, plus being this close to a place beyond her wildest dreams. There was a small window in the door at eye level. Four metal bars cross-hatched the window, reminding her of a prison cell. Terrified all over again, she kicked at him and tried to throw herself to the side.

"Not going to happen!" His hand closed around the chain inches from her throat and he all but lifted her off her feet. "Believe me, I know what I'm doing."

Desperate for air, she twisted about as he opened the door. He stepped behind her and shoved, causing her to sprawl belly down on thick carpet. He slammed and locked the door then stepped on the chain so she couldn't lift her head.

"This isn't the introduction to my place I'd intended, but thanks for the reminder of our relationship."

Try as she did, she couldn't look up at him. Carpet fibers pressed against her mouth and eyes.

"All right, let's get something straight. We're going to do things my way, my purpose." He paused. "I've never brought a subject here, so, in that respect, I'm in uncharted territory, but, have no doubt, I know what I'm doing."

Subject? What is he talking about?

She relaxed a little as he lifted his foot off the chain, but then he slid his hands under the belt at her back. He almost effortlessly lifted her onto her feet. As long as her hands had been tied to her middle, she should've been used to it, so why did her fingers keep clenching and unclenching?

"This isn't set up to be a training facility, but the possibilities and potential intrigue me. It'll give me purpose." He still had hold of the belt so she had no choice but to stand in place. She took note of horizontally placed logs that made up the walls and filtered light from the windows, but was too overwhelmed to concentrate on what he'd said.

"Training," he muttered. "Yeah, I guess so."

He seemed to be talking more to himself than her so she ignored him as best she could, in large part because she feared his words would tip her back into insanity.

"Possibilities, possibilities," he continued. "Let me think. I didn't expect…"

This man liked strawberry ice cream and lived in a place she could've only dreamed of, set in the middle of a beautiful wilderness. How could he be this — this monster?

The longer she waited for him to make a decision that might forever alter the course of her life, the more she became aware of her exhaustion and empty stomach. She was getting even more lightheaded.

"To state what might be the obvious," he said, "I don't have neighbors. My property is on the west side of a small lake. There are a couple of cabins on the east side, but I own five acres and the others respect boundary lines. Electricity comes from a generator and I use wood heat. Fortunately, there's satellite so I'm able to keep in touch with…"

Fighting her weakness, she focused on her surroundings. A wide, wooden staircase led up to the second story. She could make out an open area at the top of the stairs and a couple of doors leading to, what? The room they were in was expansive, with a stone fireplace ahead of her, a large-screen TV to the left and a sitting area with a leather couch and recliner to the right. Man cave, she concluded. The kitchen was beyond where they were and there were a couple of other rooms she couldn't see into.

The longer she surveyed her surroundings, the more they enveloped her. Lantern-like lighting hung from the maybe fifteen foot high ceiling and several sets of deer antlers were on the walls. She shuddered at the thought of her captor killing a buck and cutting the rack off the carcass.

Maybe, she told herself, he'd found the antlers while wandering around.

Wood dominated, and as she acknowledged the massive pillars and whole wood walls, the more intimidated she became. The trailer she'd inherited along with her summer job had been claustrophobic while this — this was masculine to the extreme.

"I don't understand." She hated, but couldn't help her frightened tone. "What is this about?"

He stared at her but didn't answer. For a moment, she believed he didn't know how to respond, but that couldn't be.

"You're mine," he muttered. "You belong to me."

"No! Please, you can't mean— Look, you need help. I'll—"

"Shut up."

Chapter Five

His command was a drumbeat, a blow to her heart. Back when a juvenile detention officer had locked her inside a cell, the officer had told her she was being locked up since that's how society dealt with those who broke the law. She had been a law-abiding citizen since her release, damn it. Her debt to society, not that she really had a debt, had been paid, her lesson learned. What merciful god would do this to her?

A moan pushed past her lips.

"Don't do this!" He jerked down on the chain until she was staring at the carpet. "Damn it, I don't need..."

He marched her, bent over, to where the stairs began, threaded the chain through a wooden railing, and clipped her in place.

She wanted to kill him, to stomp him and stomp him, make him admit she was a human and not some animal. Instead, she stood where he'd placed her.

He ran his hands over her, starting with her neck, moving over her immobile arms, down her sides, over her hips, along her thighs. To her disbelief, she relaxed a little.

"There are going to be a lot of rules," he told her. "Some I intend to spell out now. Others will come along later. To some extent, how I treat you depends on how well you obey my commands, understand?"

"Why?"

He clamped his fingers around her chin and forced her to look up at him. "Rule number one, you don't ask questions. Why this is happening is no concern of yours, you simply need to learn. Obey. Become."

'Are you going to kill me?' she longed to ask but he'd made it clear she wasn't to ask questions. Maybe if she played along with his sick game —

"Rule number two, I call the shots. All of them. Whatever I tell you to do, you do it. Every time I decide to hurt you, it'll happen."

Hurt? More than he already had?

"I'm stronger than you, not that I need to point that out. In addition, I know how to use my strength. How to intimidate and control. To mold."

He'd massaged her thighs, spelling out his crazy rules, his light touch standing in sharp contrast to his words. Having his fingers so close to her shorts hem was unnerving, but anything was better than being tied to a truck bed. Maybe.

"This isn't a rule so much as a promise." He slipped his fingers under her shorts and aimed at the gap between her legs. "You're going to become something you never imagined was possible. Initially, you'll find the transformation both terrifying and painful, but even then, there'll be certain rewards. I'll parcel those out when it pleases me to do so and they do the most good." His fingers were closing in on her panties crotch. How could he expect her to concentrate on anything else?

"Your body will undergo a transformation. No matter what happens during the rest of your life, my lessons will remain imprinted on you. You'll both love and hate your body. The love — for lack of a better term — will come from sexual pleasure, but you'll hate a great deal about the process, in large part because you'll have no control over it." He chuckled. "There's also a not small issue of discomfort."

She'd vowed not to look down at what his hands were doing but couldn't stop herself. Expressionless, he faced her squarely while his fingers continued their relentless approach toward her sex. Her legs throbbed with the desire to kick or knee him, but if she did, he'd punish her. Teach her the true meaning of pain.

"You have impressive self-control." Something, his thumb

maybe, swept over the bit of fabric between him and her pussy. She shivered. "Most subjects can't hold it together, particularly at the beginning."

"How many—" She clamped her teeth together. Had she stopped the question in time?

"How many subjects have I done this to? I don't remember."

That couldn't be! Could it?

"I'm going to try something, a bit of a test."

The way he'd framed his words, she was certain he intended to force his fingers into her, so was unprepared when he abruptly withdrew and stepped back. His bulk blocked her view of the door she couldn't escape through, and her right shoulder pressed against the stair post. The only way she could decrease the pressure around her neck was by leaning toward the post, but that would put her off balance.

"How responsive are you?" he asked. "Does it take much to turn you on?"

No. If she told him the truth, he'd use his knowledge to his advantage. Shaking, she struggled to return his gaze.

"Answer me!" He slapped her cheek, knocking her head to the side. A moment later, he grabbed her shorts waistband and yanked them down so they were around her knees. "Unless you want a repeat of that particular lesson, I strongly suggest you tell me the truth."

Knowing it was useless, she nevertheless strained to free her arms. "I-I don't know how to answer."

"The hell you don't."

She steeled herself for another slap, but he tightened the chain so she faced the post with her nose touching it. He was behind her.

Getting ready to what?

"I've changed my mind," he told her. "I suspect you won't come clean about your responsiveness, not the truth, anyway. Far better for me to figure it out on my own."

His hands settled on her hips. Alarm ratcheted up,

compelling her to try to look over her shoulder. Everything was happening too fast. Was too intense.

"A key element in the training process," he said, "is demonstrating to a subject that I can and will do whatever I want. There's nothing she can do to stop me. Think about your current predicament. Your restraints aren't elaborate. In fact, they're much simpler than they'll be down the road, but they do the job. To state the obvious, I have you right where I want you."

"You don't have to do this. It isn't too late to stop. I don't know where we are, who you are. Just let me go and I'll never —"

"I know what you're doing, slave. You're mentally bargaining with me. Appealing to my civilized nature and compassion." His fingers dug in. "Save your breath. Pleas and promises have no impact on me."

Slave. He just called me a slave.

"All right." He leaned into her, pulled her top off her shoulder, and lightly bit the just-exposed flesh. She whimpered. "Back to the issue at hand, which, as I recall, was my goal of assessing what it takes to turn your body against you." He straightened. A moment later his fingers again dug into her buttocks. "I care how long it takes me to make that determination. In fact, I'm looking forward to the journey. To anything."

Was there something wistful about the way he'd said the last? Before she could go in search of an answer, he drew her panties down to her shorts. She'd known he'd eventually strip off her clothes, but it was happening too fast.

Scaring her too much.

Taking her a million miles from the erotic scenarios she'd long let run rampant in her mind.

"Not bad." He patted her now naked ass cheeks. "Obviously, you live an active lifestyle. I'd prefer it if you had an all-over tan, but maybe I'll make that happen."

Tans took time. Time she'd have to spend in his presence. Alive.

As his slave.

"Always before," he continued, "I made a point of not giving a slave any information about the process, as we call it at Carnal, but at present, my employer has nothing to do with you and me. Maybe it never will. I can change things up, maybe share some…"

Try as she did, she couldn't concentrate on what he was saying. Something about Carnal, whatever that was. He'd demonstrated his capacity for delivering pain, but that wasn't the only reason she felt as if she were drowning. His hands were where no stranger had the right to place them. He'd stripped her — begun to, anyway.

And she couldn't do anything to stop him.

"The woman's body is endlessly fascinating." His nails raked her buttocks, making her jump and gasp. "I know more about the female form than the majority of men, and yet, I'm always learning something new. Keeps me from getting bored."

He'd thrown too much at her, overloaded her mind and nerves. He'd snugged her tightly to the post, but she again struggled to see what he was doing.

Strong, smooth nails dug into the bottom of her buttocks. Gasping, she rose onto her toes, but, of course, he stayed with her. Kept the pressure going. All too soon her calves were trembling. Short moments later, she sank back down again. His nails continued to dig at her. Sharp pain bloomed. She stamped her feet then began to bend her left knee.

"No, slave, no! Don't even think it."

A fist pushed into the small of her back and forced her hard against the post. Her breasts were being smashed, her useless hands on wood.

"I will teach you the meaning of the word pain, but there are things you can do to limit the amount of discomfort I believe it's necessary to subject you to. I'll grant you that one option. The last thing you ever want to do is try to inflict damage on me. Believe me, you'll regret it as you've never regretted anything in your life. Do you understand me?"

He expected her to answer?

"Ah, a bit of defiance." The pressure at the small of her back increased until it reached her core. "I must say that's always been the most rewarding thing about working with a new slave." He nipped the side of her neck. "You're going to try to escape. I'd be disappointed and surprised if you didn't." He again settled his teeth over her neck like some vampire. "I'm curious to see what you do, or rather, I should say, attempt to do. Carnal—maybe I'll show you pictures of the various facilities—is designed to keep captives under control. To bring up the obvious, it's different here. I don't have any cages."

Cages. Cells. Despite her effort to hide her fear from him, a whimper slipped past her clenched teeth.

He sighed. "Taking you was…something I needed to do to keep from losing my mind." He took a deep breath. "From thinking too much."

Her fantasy captor never explained himself. Everything revolved around her needs, her maybe sick desires. She didn't want to know anything about this flesh and blood man—and yet her survival depended on it.

"All right, slave-in-training, it's time I got back to why I've restrained you the way I have. Besides—"

Not for the first time, he'd stopped himself from revealing something. Somehow, some way she'd have to get him to tell her more, but not now. Not yet.

When he stopped mashing her against the post, she came too close to thanking him. Not trusting her control, she resisted trying to see what he was doing. The seconds ticked past. She couldn't stop shaking.

"Lovely responses." Warm hands settled over her buttocks. "You have no idea how many men want total control over a woman who lives in fear of him and will do whatever it takes to please him. And to bring herself pleasure. The majority of men never have the opportunity to experience that, of course, but a few do." He kneaded her too-pliable flesh. "However, enough have the necessary finances to make Carnal Incorporated highly successful."

Right now, he wasn't hurting her. That was all she could think about, his potential for gentleness. His quiet words. And the word 'Carnal'.

"You're a wild animal," he whispered. "One I've caught in my trap. Unlike a creature of the forest, you're intelligent enough to know not to exhaust yourself fighting what can't be fought."

As the kneading sensation continued, she became aware of several changes. For one, his fingers were slowly heading down toward her thighs. Number two, the touches were becoming gentler. She was so tired, so out of her element.

And she wanted…something.

"Fear isn't a static emotion," he continued. "Even in the middle of a life-threatening experience, human beings can't indefinitely remain on high alert. Nerves can only take so much before they demand a break or start breaking down."

His take-charge fingers settled fully over the backs of her thighs. She shivered, experienced.

"So soft. What was I saying? Oh, yes, during our period of togetherness, there will be any number of times you're convinced you can't take any more, shall we call it, stimulation, but I encourage you to face your fears and desires rather than hiding from them. Your unconscious mind and nerves know what needs to be done. Each time you find yourself about to fall off an emotional cliff into madness or absolute surrender, hold on for a few more seconds. You'll slip into another realm. It'll get better once you're there. Marginally."

Why was he throwing this nonsense at her? And what did he mean by their period of togetherness? How long would it last?

His breathing picked up and became deeper. Between trying to anticipate his next move and facing her new reality, she'd already forgotten most of what he'd said.

"I'm looking forward to this, to blazing my own path instead of following Carnal's dictates. Who knows?

Maybe…"

She hated it when he fell silent. She was so damn weak. At the same time, strength she couldn't begin to make use of surged through her in waves.

"It's catching up to me," he said abruptly. "Damn, damn."

"What is?"

"Did I give you permission to speak?" He sounded more disappointed than angry. "One more outburst like that and I'll gag you again." Masculine fingers slipped between her thighs. A moment later something, a nail from the feel of it, brushed her clit. Sweat broke out all over. She longed to leave this life and return to the one she'd created.

One safer than this.

At the same time, she'd never been more alive, more aware of her body.

"Hold still now. No matter what I do, you aren't to move."

She was so tense she half expected her bones to crack, her muscles to shatter. Whatever he intended was taking so damn long. Damn him to Hell.

"The sweet spot. And your undoing."

He touched her sex again. Even though she had no doubt what he was going to do, she couldn't ignore the sweep of masculine fingers along her pussy lips. Teeth clenched, she concentrated on breathing.

"Listen to your body. Hear what it's saying to you, slave."

Slave? No!

Maybe, yes.

Yet another light touch of male fingers over her private female body parts. Her partly discarded clothes pressed against her knees. She tried to close her legs.

"No!" He pulled one hand free, slid it under her top, and raked her back from shoulder to buttocks. "This is my right. You're my possession."

She wasn't anyone's possession, hadn't been under anyone's control since she'd turned eighteen. Not ready to tell her captor that, she struggled to ride out the stinging sensations along her spine. They'd barely begun to fade when he ran a finger into her sex opening. Alarmed and insanely excited, she froze.

"Do you remember what I called this place?" He wiggled his finger.

A question, something she needed to answer. "My... sweet spot."

"What else?"

She couldn't give him what he was demanding, damn him! Sweat ran down her sides. Cracks formed in her mind. She felt...good.

"Don't try my patience, slave. I'm not a patient man."

He hadn't repeated his question. She desperately held on to this moment, this small victory. He must have known what she was doing—maybe he knew everything about her—because, instead of screaming at her, he pushed deeper into her.

"You're damp up here, little one. Not as wet as you're capable of becoming, but it's a start. Stay with me. Experience."

This man who'd already done countless things he had no right doing began playing with her. That's what it was, she repeatedly told herself, teasing and playing. Crude foreplay. He used both hands to spread her as far as the fabric roping her knees allowed. Whistling—whistling!—he dipped one finger after another into her and used what he collected to coat her labial lips.

She hated noting everything he was doing, but she had no choice. The need to try to stay one half-step ahead of him was that strong. Tension upon tension packed around her and took her down into a dark, hot place.

He wasn't hurting her. In fact, nothing in the light brushing of flesh on flesh hinted that he might. In essence, he kept after her. His fingers spoke to that primal part of her, slipped past the fragmented defenses she'd tried to throw up between them. Her captor knew to stroke and feather, how deep to climb into her, how long to stay there.

Anxiety seeped out of her, and, moment by moment, she

71

relaxed. He was working her slow, slow and light, gentle. Knowing.

"That's better," he muttered. "No need to think it's all going to be bad. It isn't."

Something stroked her channel walls. More curious than alarmed, she concentrated. Two of his fingers were inside her now. Claiming ownership. Giving pleasure.

"More moisture, my pet." He pushed up, slid out a little, advanced again. "I'm milking you. It's as simple as that."

"Hmm." She couldn't feel anything except this one part of her body.

"Repeat for me, slave. What am I doing?"

So good. Knowing and compassionate fingers taking her to a place empty of fear. Maybe…maybe he'd help her climax.

"You…you're stimulating me."

He wiggled his fingers. "What else?"

"Oh…I…don't know what you want me to say."

"It sounds as if self-analysis isn't possible for you right now. All right, go back inside yourself and listen to your cunt."

Sweat now ran off her temples. Her forehead hurt from leaning against the post. Pressure where thigh and pussy joined let her know he'd brought his other hand back into play. Two fingers continued to lay claim to her sex opening, held her open and vulnerable. Filled her. Much as she needed to stomp down on her body's response, she couldn't. He'd taken hold of a labial lip and was pulling on it, stretching tender flesh. He'd covered her in her own juices there and had to hold on so tightly that circulation was being cut off. Burning, heat rising, discomfort mating with pleasure.

"Hmm, mmm."

"Music to my ears, slave. It's a devil's dance, isn't it? Give me more. Fall apart for me."

No! You can't make me —

He rammed his fingers so deeply into her she half believed

she could taste them. For a blessed few seconds, he let go of her sex lips. Then, before circulation was fully restored, he grabbed hold again. She couldn't begin to compare this pinching, clamping sensation with what was going on inside her. It was all so much. Overwhelming.

"Please, oh, God, please."

"There's no god here, slave. Never was, never will be."

She knew that, but the word had escaped, anyway.

"A little more and then I need to...damn."

Was he in pain again? She was the one who was—was what? Her body was beyond her reach or control, drifting between good and bad. Wonderful and hated. Holding her breath, she tried to concentrate on the good. He hadn't touched her clit lately, but she forgave him because his fingers provided what her pussy craved. Her captor had skewered her, invaded that private and fragile place. Maybe, hopefully, his attack would continue until she lost all awareness of her tethered hands, the tight leather around her waist, the collar.

Her pussy wasn't selective. Almost any stimulation between her legs would get her off. Left to her own devices, she got down to basics by pressing a vibrator to her clit but—

Where had she gone? How had she managed to dismiss the punishing fingers clamped around her sex lip for even a second?

"Shit, mmm, shit."

"What's that, slave? I can't hear you."

More pressure. Her pussy flesh being relentlessly pulled. Desperate to escape, she twisted one way and the other. It did her no good. He was still there, fingers clinging to her and inside her, his larger body looming behind her.

"Oh, please. Oh, shit, please stop!"

"Begging won't get you anywhere, slave. Ever. Get used to it."

She couldn't, especially not with two powerful male hands between her thighs. Claiming her sex. Owning her.

"What do you want? Oh, G— What do you want?"

"Your surrender."

No! Never. She kept twisting, fighting what couldn't be fought. "Damn, damn, damn you."

Someone was grunting. At first, she thought she was responsible for the harsh sounds, then realized they were coming from him. Sensing that her sanity and maybe her life might depend on what she did now, she forced herself to stop her useless struggle. Between his grunts and her rapid-fire panting, they sounded like a couple of boxers at the end of a match. Her pussy was on fire, invaded by an overwhelming mix of what was good and bad about her body. Her rock-like nipples pressed against her bra, and she couldn't close her mouth.

"Enough," he said. "Shit, enough."

His fingers slid out of her. The awful-wonderful sensation on her labia eased then died. She dimly realized he'd backed away, but couldn't concentrate on him, not unless her body mended itself. Found a moment of peace.

It happened one nerve ending at a time. Finally, she no longer stood at the edge of a cliff. Sometimes, when her directionless life became more than she wanted to think about, she engaged in a long night of self-stimulation. Climaxing over and over again wiped her mind clean and left her tired and satisfied. She was a little like that now, which shouldn't have been, since there'd been nothing pleasurable about what her captor had subjected her to. Her reaction had to be, she told herself, a combination of fear and helplessness.

The pressure around her neck lessened, allowing her to stand upright and swivel toward her captor. His nostrils were slightly flared and he was squinting. Harsh lines between his eyes, coupled with his clenched jaw, made her conclude that he was in pain. He grabbed her chin and forced her head to the side.

"What I'm dealing with is none of your concern, got it? I pushed myself more than I should have, that's all." He briefly closed his eyes then shook his head, as if trying to reconcile himself to what he'd just revealed.

She waited him out because she had no choice and sure as hell wasn't going to express sympathy. He'd hurt her, not the other way around.

But had he really caused her pain? She couldn't say.

"I'm going to catch a nap," he said, almost conversationally. "But before I do I need to park you so you won't get into mischief."

Still neck-tethered to the post, she watched as he slowly walked away from her and through a door to the left of the living room. She felt ridiculous and exposed standing there with her clothes hobbling her and her ass sticking out. He was going to rape her. It was just a matter of time. Over and over again until he grew tired of her then—

Slave. He'd called her a slave.

His sex slave?

She stared at the door until it opened again. He was carrying a length of rope. Something bulged from his jeans pocket. If anything, his pace was even slower and was he dragging his left leg a little? Maybe it was her imagination, but his lips looked paler than earlier.

A fresh wave of helplessness struck her as he wrapped the new rope around what was already on her wrists. After he'd secured her to his satisfaction, he released her arms from the belt and drew them down so her hands were against her mons.

"To state the obvious," he said, "I strongly suggest you not fight me. You might believe I'm at a bit of a disadvantage right now." He ran his hand over his left thigh. "But I'm still stronger than you. Besides"—he slapped her cheek—"you don't want to make me angry."

The blow didn't sting as much as the earlier ones had, but she got the message. She wouldn't resist, at least not now.

To her shock, he threaded the loose end of the new rope between her legs and drew it upward so the strands settled on her crack. Positioned the way she was, she couldn't see what he was securing the rope to behind her, something so high he had to strain to reach it. He tugged, forcing her arms even lower and making her lean over. Cotton connected with her pussy.

He stepped away from her. "That should hold you. It won't be comfortable. In fact, the longer you have to stand there, the greater the strain." The corners of his mouth lifted. "Think on the reasons behind my actions while you wait for me to return. It'll help you pass the time."

He extended his hand toward her. She winced and tried to move away. He patted her cheek.

"Sometimes I want to hear a subject's vocalizations, sometimes I don't. Right now, I want it quiet here." He frowned. "I didn't have to tell you that, I could simply..."

Still frowning, he reached into his pocket and withdrew a red rubber ball with leather straps attached to it. Having seen several online BDSM sites, she recognized it as a gag.

"Don't make this any harder than it needs to be," he told her. "Depending on my mood, I get turned on when a subject struggles, but this isn't one of those times."

I hate you, I hate you, she chanted as he pressed the ball into her mouth. Once it was in as far as it would go, he fastened the straps at the back of her neck with her hair trapped under the leather. She started drooling so shook her head, trying to dislodge it.

"Fight it if you want to, but I suggest you save your energy. Believe me, every time I gag a slave she stays gagged."

'Slave'. That word again.

He unsnapped the chain from her collar but left it dangling from the post. After studying her for a moment, he ran his hand from her wrists to her fingers.

"Your circulation's intact. Fight this little contraption I've set up and the rope will dig into you more than it already is. In other words, the amount of discomfort you experience while I'm gone is entirely up to you." He slid a hand over her inner thigh, pushed up on the strands flattening her labial lips. She whimpered into the gag.

"Not the most enjoyable thing that's ever happened to your pussy, but that, too, is part of today's lesson." He withdrew, took hold of her hips, and turned her away from him. "That's what I thought," he muttered. "A little adjustment needed here."

Her head sagged and she repeatedly tightened and relaxed her fingers as he repositioned the rope so it was between her ass cheeks. He slapped her right buttock, then her left, the right again, followed by the left.

She didn't want to move, damn it. He wasn't hitting her that hard, more a tease than a spanking, so why did she jump and fight her bondage with every blow?

"I'll return." He grabbed the rope and jerked up, forcing her onto her toes. "That'll give you something else to think about—I will return."

By the time her captor started up the stairs, she was exhausted. His footsteps faded, letting her know she was alone.

He'd secured the rope against her pussy and asshole to a high stair railing. If she had use of her arms, she could have reached up and untied it, but of course he'd made that impossible.

She couldn't call for help, couldn't move from where he'd placed her. Tight as the bonds were, she couldn't straighten. Until he returned, her sex would remain trapped and sensitive. Her shorts and briefs were still around her knees.

He could and would do whatever he wanted with her for as long as he wanted.

She belonged to him.

Chapter Six

By the time he reached the loft, where his bedroom was, Reno had reconciled himself to taking a prescription pain pill. Damn it, except for the occasional night, he'd been able to stay off the heavy stuff. Of course, he unnecessarily reminded himself as he went into the adjacent bathroom, he hadn't asked this much of his body since before the accident.

After swallowing the pill and using the toilet, he kicked off his shoes and eased onto the bed. He didn't pull a blanket over him. If he was too comfortable who knew how long he'd sleep, and he didn't want to damage the merchandise.

He'd given in to crazy impulse, brought a captive here.

Captive? Not a slave-in-training?

Damn it, he wasn't going to let stupid word choices get between him and a nap. He was what he was, and she was...something.

What was her name?

Why had he brought her to his retreat, his place of peace?

And what was he going to do with her?

* * * *

"You want the truth? I'm not surprised."

Resisting the urge to hold his cell phone away from his ear so he could glare at it, Reno mentally replayed what his co-worker had just said. He and Damek had begun working for Carnal around the same time, and had collaborated on several slave trainings. Damek had been the first person to come see him in the hospital, the only one to show up more than once. More importantly, Damek's expression had said he realized something had changed about his co-worker, but he knew not to press the issue.

"What's she like?" Damek asked. "I take it you chose someone without a support system and with the qualities we look for."

We? What about me?

"I don't know much about her," he admitted. He'd been somewhere between asleep and awake when Damek had called and was still trying to get with the program. "You've done it yourself. You come across a broad with the submissive qualities you're looking for and know it."

"What makes you think she's submissive?"

"I know, damn it."

Damek chuckled. "Yeah, you do. I'll hand you that. So, you brought her to the cabin. That surprises me."

Me too. "What else could I to do with her, keep her in some damn motel? Maybe rent an apartment and hope the neighbors don't hear?"

"You didn't have to grab her."

No, he didn't. "Go to hell."

"Don't get on my case. I'm just pointing out the obvious." Damek cleared his throat. "No, I'm doing more than that. The cabin's your sanctuary. What is it you told me, that you never bring anyone from Carnal there because you don't believe in mixing your business and personal lives?"

"You've been here."

"Yeah."

As he waited for his fellow slave trainer to say something, he picked up his shoes, only to drop them and reach for his slippers. Going by the clock near the headboard, he figured he'd slept about an hour. His body was humming, proof that the pain pill had kicked in. He was still a little groggy, but that was fading.

"I picked up on some gossip involving you," Damek said. "Sounds like you agreed to take a look at a couple of new hires. Were you coming back from that when you grabbed her?"

"Yeah. What did management say?"

"A couple of things. You look better than they thought you would."

"What was the other thing?" he asked, even though he was pretty sure he knew.

"Paul and Dwight both asked what drugs you were on. They said you acted like you didn't give a damn about the operation. You didn't ask about the improvements going on at the West facility."

"Right now I don't care," he admitted. He trusted Damek to keep his mouth shut. Otherwise, he wouldn't have said a word. "Management asked me to comment on the two apprentices and that's what I did. I told them to get rid of one who's a damn sadist. The other has possibilities."

"For the record," Damek said, "they took your advice. The last thing Carnal needs is a trainer who ruins the merchandise. By the way, management asked me if you'd mentioned coming back to work. We need you."

"I'm not ready." He rubbed his leg.

"Physically or emotionally?"

"Go to hell."

Damek sighed. "That's what I thought. Maybe grabbing her is proof that you're getting ready to get back in the saddle."

"Maybe."

Working for Carnal Incorporated paid more bills than anything else he'd ever done, not that he had much of a résumé. All of the facilities were first class, and, for the most part, he could pick his jobs. As for the work itself — hell, what man wouldn't want to spend his life pawing an endless succession of naked females?

Maybe him.

"What are you going to do with her?" Damek asked.

He didn't have to tell his co-worker anything. If he again told Damek to go to hell that would be the end of things. Their friendship would continue. He simply wouldn't step over that particular line. But Damek was the only person on this earth he ever let down his hair around.

"I haven't decided. I'm playing this one step at a time."

"So you saw her, picked up some vibes, and decided to grab her?"

"Something like that."

"Hell, it isn't that simple and we both know it. Don't damage the merchandise."

"I don't intend to." He wasn't sure he meant it. Maybe if he broke her into little pieces and fashioned her into the ultimate sex slave, he'd stop asking himself who and what she was and why he wanted her in his life.

"Anything you want me to tell management?"

Good question. One he needed to answer. "I'm not sure." Disgusted with himself, he stood and walked over to the door. Once this conversation was over with, he'd open it, go down the stairs, and—and what? "Tell them there's been a complication."

"That's what this broad is to you, a complication?"

"I don't know."

But I need to find out.

* * * *

He was wearing slippers.

If her captor had asked why she'd noted that, Kaci wasn't sure she'd have been able to explain. Maybe the whispery sound made her think he was stalking her. Maybe he appeared less intimidating this way.

She hurt and yet she didn't. Every nerve in her immobile body was on high alert, which reminded her of what it had had been like to stare out of a cell window at a spring morning and know she wouldn't feel the sun on her back today.

No! She wouldn't cry, wouldn't beg. Would get through this just as she'd survived her stint as a juvenile delinquent.

And her childhood.

"You have to pee."

Her captor hadn't said anything when he'd first rejoined her. After descending the stairs, he'd planted himself near her right side. Even though she hadn't looked at him—ignoring him was her only defiant act—she had no choice but to face what he was seeing.

Helpless and partly naked female flesh.

He snorted and yanked on the rope between her legs, making her squeal. "Let's get something straight, slave. Every time I ask a question, you will respond to the best of your ability. I know how to get the truth out of someone. Your choice—either it goes easy or hard."

Damn him! He didn't have a single speck of humanity in him. Angry, she faced him and jerked her head up and down.

"What's that?"

Fuck you. The emotion under control, she made her expression neutral.

"I know what it is." He tapped her cheek. "You'd like nothing more than to see me in Hell." Again, he patted the side of her face, forcing her to concentrate on not shying away. "Interesting. I thought you'd be more scared than pissed." He slipped a finger under the strap that held the gag in place. "Your attitude is giving me something new to think about, to examine while I work with you."

Was that excitement? And he was again making it clear that this wasn't the first time he'd had someone under his control.

Had her fantasies come to life? If so, she was doing a piss poor job of fashioning them to meet her secret needs.

"All right." His finger still hard on her jaw, he moved so he was directly in front of her. Bent the way she was, he loomed over her. "Here's how we're going to get going. First off, I'll haul you into the bathroom. Otherwise, things will get messy and I don't want that. So far, I've been easy on you, but it's time for your training to begin."

Easy? What a lie that was.

He planted his hands on her shoulders and pushed her back. Her bare ass pressed against the post. The punishing rope tightened, forcing her onto her toes. Drool dripped. If not for the restraints, she would have fallen forward. Even more disconcerting was the added warmth to her pussy. No way had the pressure and his presence turned her on.

No way!

"This serves as a quick lesson. I already made it clear that I have thorough knowledge of how a female's body works, but, in case you've forgotten, here's the reminder. Keep that foremost in mind while we dispense with the essentials."

Years ago, she'd attended classes held at the juvenile facility. For the most part, she'd hated them because the teacher had aimed the lessons at the slowest students and his delivery had been so dry she'd often fallen asleep. In some respects, what her captor had just said took her back to that time. Why did he think he had to warn her about anything? He was in control of everything.

"This place has two bathrooms." He was doing something to the rope behind and above her. "Maybe eventually I'll let you use my personal one, maybe not. I haven't decided."

The tension between her legs ended. Off balance, she stumbled forward. By the time she was standing upright, he'd pulled the rope off her sex. He held it in front of her. A sharp tug yanked her arms up.

"There." He jerked his head toward another closed door. "Get your ass over there and you won't get into any more trouble than you're already in."

His harsh chuckle cut through her, nibbled at the anger that had been sustaining her. Resigned, she started after him, only to have to slow to an awkward shuffle thanks to the restraining clothes around her knees. He walked with his back to her, and the hand holding the rope rested on his shoulder as if he were carrying a backpack. There wasn't that much distance between the stairs and the bathroom, but it took what seemed forever to reach it. By the time she did, her bladder all but screamed at her.

He opened the door and shoved her into the dark space. She slammed into something hard. Before her eyes could adjust, he switched on a light.

The bathroom was small with a pedestal sink, small shower, and toilet. It was paneled in wood, which made her feel as if it were closing in on her. Two people could just fit in the space and would be hard-put to maneuver around each other.

"You have choices," he said, from where he stood in the entryway. "Either you take care of business like a good little slave or I come in."

'Slave'. Belonging to him.

Seeing the toilet made everything else unimportant. Even before she sat on it, her bladder loosened. She peed and peed, her useless hands resting on her thighs. The long rope lay on her stretched shorts and the tile floor near the one attached to her ankle. After she was done, she awkwardly took hold of the toilet paper and wiped.

He'd watched, had seen her relief followed by her stumbling efforts to take care of the most basic function.

"One more thing before you get up. Let's see if you can figure out what it is."

Sick at heart, she pushed her shorts and panties to the floor and gathered up the ankle rope so she could slide it under her garments. As she stepped out of her clothes, she wondered if she'd ever wear them again.

"You're a sticky, sweaty mess but there isn't much point in cleaning you up until after today's lesson."

He'd given her permission to leave the bathroom, hadn't he? But the only place she could go was back to him. Nauseated, she fumbled with the faucet, rinsed her hands, and dried them on a plush towel. A glance at the mirror was enough. She didn't recognize the gagged woman staring back at her. Facing him and taking the necessary step made her dizzy, but she'd be damned if she'd let him know how much it took out of her.

To her discomfort, he simply stared at her for a long time.

Then, "Follow me."

How dare he expect her to trail after him like some dog! Having him overpower her using his greater strength was one thing, but expecting her to dumbly give in was too much, though they both knew she had no choice.

This time, he didn't haul her behind him but walked ahead. He didn't bother to look back at her. Feeling disconnected from reality, she concentrated on not tripping over the ropes. No doubt about it, he'd kept both in place in case he had to quickly regain control over her.

That was the kind of bastard he was.

It was beautiful outside. She'd seen enough of the peaceful setting that it called to her. A quick twist of the doorknob and she'd —

He stopped in the middle of the living room. His slow pace as he faced her made her wonder if he'd had to talk himself into it, but that was crazy. Head cocked to the side, he crooked a finger at her, indicating that he wanted her to come closer.

"I haven't decided on my ultimate use for you," he informed her when she was so close his masculine heat enveloped her. "Regardless, your transformation will remain the same." He pointed at the room where he had gone for the rope. "I could have already brought out everything I'll need for this lesson, but if I had, you'd be focusing on the instruments, not me."

Don't say those things!

"First up, some modifications in your restraints. While we're at it, it's time we got rid of this." His hand snaked out and he grabbed her top's neckline. "Where'd you get this damn thing, some yard sale?"

Alarmed as she was, she couldn't think of what she was wearing, but she seldom bought new so he was probably right. She started to lean away but stopped when he made it clear he wasn't going to let go. Smiling, he pulled her against him. He had an erection.

They stood body to body, heat to heat with their expelled

breaths merging. He wasn't a massive man, some six to eight inches taller than her, older but not that much. In other circumstances, she might have been drawn to the masculinity radiating from his core. This man took charge. Nothing intimidated him. The women in his life would never doubt that they'd be cared for.

She had to be going crazy! Otherwise, she'd never think that.

Never let her stupid submissive fanaticizing mess with reality.

"Here's the drill, slave. The only thing you have to do right now is stand there. I'll take care of everything."

Her jaw had gone numb from the ball gag. Even if he took it out, she wasn't sure she could speak. Besides, what would she say? Obviously, pleas and promises wouldn't work with him. She could ask if he intended to kill her, but did she want to know and could she believe anything he said?

On a sigh, he pushed her away, letting go of her top as he did. She grunted but didn't move when he took hold of the rope around her wrists and began untying the knots. Once he'd freed the lead, he wrapped it over his shoulder and worked on the strands that had long rendered her hands useless.

"How's your circulation? Anything feel compromised?"

Wondering if he cared at all about her comfort, she rubbed one wrist then the other. She was aware of the indentations the loops had left in her skin, but, surprisingly, there was little tingling.

"Nope. Haven't lost my touch. All right, you have two choices. Either I strip you or you do it."

To hell with him! No way would she play his sick game. She tightened her muscles in preparation for making a run for the door.

"No you don't!" A masculine hand snaked out and grabbed the ring in her collar, yanking down and forcing her onto her hands and knees. He knelt beside her and rolled her onto her back. Then he straddled her, his weight settled over her naked belly.

"Want to wrestle, do you? There's nothing I'd like more than to accommodate you."

Despite her frantic struggles, he easily placed her arms over her head. He released them, but before she could bring them back down, he grabbed her top's hem and yanked up. The garment snagged on the damnable collar and the gag. All too soon, he'd torn it off her.

"Round one goes to me."

Screaming into the horrible ball, she reached for his face, thinking to bury her nails in his flesh. However, he clamped his hand under her chin just above the collar. She couldn't breathe.

"Not going to happen, slave. Not fucking going to happen."

Her vision blurred, and her arms became so weak she couldn't make them work. He was killing her. Destroying her.

In a vague and uninterested way, she knew she was passing out. At first, not being able to breathe terrified her. Then it became unimportant. Any second now, the nightmare would end. She'd be done. Dead.

"Got the point, did you?"

Blessed fresh air filled her lungs. He was lifting himself off her, but trying to determine his intentions would have to wait until she was clearheaded.

Not giving her time, he rolled her onto her stomach, settled himself over her ass, and drew her hands behind her. He used a just-discarded rope to secure her wrists to the belt's ring in the back, ensuring that she wouldn't have another chance to try to attack him. After he was done, he took hold of her elbows and lifted her upper body off the floor. He was still sitting on her buttocks which meant her back was deeply bowed.

A sob escaped past the gag.

"Not quite as cocky as you were, are you? We're just

getting started."

She tried to tell herself he was simply torturing her with his words, that he wasn't a monster. Then he got off her and she rolled to the side as much as her deeply bent elbows allowed and looked up at him.

The way he glared down at her reminded her of a predator standing over his prey.

"On your feet, slave."

Her throat still hurt from where he'd squeezed it, but that didn't bother her as much as realizing he'd heard her cry. She wasn't sure why staying strong was so important, just that not emotionally surrendering was all she had.

Naked except for ropes, leather, and her bra, she forced her knees under her. She tried to stand, but, without her arms for balance, she fell forward.

"Keep at it, slave. If you haven't succeeded by the time I return, you'll pay the price."

He was walking away, heading for the room she feared was filled with instruments of torture. Despite that, being alone helped settle her enough that she managed to formulate a plan. Scooting across the room on her knees was hard, but finally she reached the closest recliner. She braced an elbow against the arm and pushed herself onto her feet.

"If I didn't know better," he said, "I'd think you were in a hurry for the lesson to begin."

How long had he been standing in the doorway? Maybe he'd witnessed her awkward and demeaning struggle. After facing him, she stood with her legs widespread, waiting—for what?

Oh, God, what was in the canvas bag he was carrying?

"Trapped, aren't you?" Looking as if he had all the time in the world to do this one thing, he studied her. His expression had changed from contemplation to all-knowing. All-powerful. "It has to be damn frustrating to know you'd have an equal chance, well, at least some kind of chance, if not for what I've placed around your wrists.

Maybe you could gouge out my eyes or knee me where a man never wants to be kneed." He reached into the bag and withdrew a short knife. "Maybe you'd bury this in me."

He started toward her.

Biting down on the miserable gag, she backpedaled.

"You don't want to do that, slave. Making me mad or frustrated will only get you in even more trouble."

She knew, she just hadn't been able to silence the instinct for survival. Reminding herself that, even though she was his prey he hadn't crippled her, she forced herself to stand her ground. The knife was a prop, something he'd use to intimidate her, not a killing weapon.

The contemplative look returned. "You interest me. More than I thought you would. There's something I don't yet have a handle on going on in that head of yours."

A compliment? Hardly.

Despite her efforts not to, she tried to twist away. He took hold of the collar ring and pulled up so she was on her toes. "Stay like that," he commanded. "Don't move a damn muscle."

She took a deep, if not calming, breath after he let go and fought to keep her legs under her. This wasn't much different from the way he'd left her to take a nap and served as yet another example of how little control she had over the situation. She needed to try to determine what he intended to do but stared at the distant and inaccessible door to freedom.

He slipped the knife under her bra between her breasts and started sawing. Too soon it parted. Her breasts were still covered but not by much. Humming, he pulled the cups off her.

Exposed. Useless scraps of material hanging off her shoulders.

"Not bad at all, and they're natural. That ups your value."

My value to whom?

Despite her effort, she couldn't remain on her toes so awkwardly settled onto the balls of her feet. She readied herself for punishment or an angry outburst, but neither came. Finally, she dared to glance down. Her breasts were exposed all right and her nipples — why were they so hard? Was fear alone responsible?

"I kind of like that look." He pulled down on the bra cups so they dangled near her armpits. "So close to modesty and yet so far. However, any clothes will get in the way of what I have planned for you so —" He waved the knife in front of her. "Hold on, slave."

Staying still while he cut through the bra straps took all her self-control. Once he'd done his damage, he yanked the ruined garment off her.

Naked. Nothing left of her life before he'd taken her. Some of her belongings in the back of his truck.

His to do what with?

"All right. What's the best way to accomplish this?" He sounded as if he were talking to himself. Shortly before he'd come back downstairs, she'd heard him talking to someone. At first, she'd thought the other person was in the cabin, then had decided he'd been on the phone. Did the man or woman on the other end of the line have any idea what his or her friend was up to? What if it was someone connected to what he'd referred to as Carnal? Maybe his co-worker was on his way here.

He again took hold of the ring and brought her back to the stairs. A fresh whimper lodged in her throat as he reattached the chain and tethered her to the railing. He hadn't left her enough room to move more than a few inches, and if she tried to look down, the collar would tighten.

After patting her right breast, he walked away. Even though she couldn't see him, her nerves warned her that he was still in the room. All too soon, he returned. A soft thud near her feet told her he'd retrieved his pack.

"They're more than all right." He settled his hands over her breasts. "At least that's how I see them, and that's what's important."

At first, he seemed content to simply cradle her boobs.

She tried to emotionally distance herself from the contact, but her nipples hardened even more. He'd given her no way to resist, not even a hint of freedom. Maybe that's what she was responding to, the ultimate in helplessness. Living at the pleasure, and under the control, of another human being.

Reality, not fantasy.

Her captor's fingers pressed against the tops of her breasts. Bit by bit the pressure increased. More alarmed than in pain, she stamped her foot.

"This is what I refer to as establishing a direct conduit between body and mind. I'm also throwing in a sensual element. I want you to remember what that feels like." His thumbs stroked her breasts' undersides. "This might be the last bit of pleasure you'll experience today, so I suggest you enjoy it as much as possible."

He was going to hurt her more than he already had. The why no longer mattered.

"Where did you come from, little slave? What were you before you became mine?"

Why was he keeping her gagged? Several times now, he'd said things that made her think he wanted to carry on a conversation, not that she'd ever do that. Having her mouth stuffed was preferable to having to speak to him— except, if she could, she might've peppered him with her own questions.

Questions like, what made him a monster?

A monster who, at the moment, was gently running knowing fingers over her too-responsive nipples.

"These are part of your undoing." He closed thumbs and forefingers around the hard nubs. "I've already brought up your weakness, so you're probably getting tired of hearing about it, but I want you to be knowledgeable about certain things." He tightened his hold, causing an electrical charge to shoot through her. "I've never wanted to do this before but…"

More pressure, the grip inescapable. Unable to concentrate

on his words, she threw herself to the side.

"Yeah," he muttered as he relaxed a little. "I don't dare ignore the possibility of negative consequences. Besides, my leg's only good for so much."

His leg, something she wasn't about to forget.

He released her throbbing nipples, and she tried to swallow, only to discover her throat was too dry. She was so hungry her stomach kept growling, but that was nothing compared to her thirst. If he intended to keep her alive, eventually he'd have to give her more to drink.

And let her rest.

He'd gotten something out of his bag while she was trying to work saliva into her throat. She risked the collar abrading her neck trying to see what he'd chosen.

More rope. Red in color and soft-looking. Draped over his shoulder.

"I want to learn everything I can about your reactions and responsiveness, which means the gag has served its purpose."

She managed not to move while he unfastened the leather at the back of her head. He pulled the ball out of her mouth. A trail of saliva hung between the gag and her lips. He caught some of the sticky moisture and rubbed it against her cheek where leather had pressed for so long.

"I believe we'll begin with a minimum of rules with regards to vocalization on your part. I won't stand for begging. Spontaneous expressions of pain are allowable. In fact, I've always considered that music to my ears. No promises, no threats, no whimpering. In other words, if the sounds you're considering making don't come from here"—he pressed against her breastbone indicating her heart—"you'd be wise to keep them to yourself."

Don't do this to me! Dear, God, please don't put me through any more. Unless...

He was waiting for a response. She nodded.

"A good start." He tossed the gag away and took the red rope off his shoulder. "Better than I expected, in fact." He shook out the length. "Most captives — by now they've lost it. You're different."

The moment he reached behind her she guessed what he had in mind. He looped strand after strand around her so the rope pressed down on the tops of her breasts. She couldn't see what he was doing. Bit by bit he was altering the way her mounds looked, adding to her captivity. After too many loops, he changed the rope's course so the strands were now under her breasts and pushing up on the swollen flesh.

"Not bad," he said, stepping back from her. "I doubt if you'll agree. What I want you to do is concentrate on how your breasts feel. Be honest. I'll know if you lie."

And you'll punish me for it. She swallowed. "It's tight. They're being pinched."

"Then I've succeeded, at least in part. A little more work and it'll be time for you to understand why I'm doing this."

He was getting something else out of the bag of horrors. Even more unsettling, he didn't let her see what it was.

His hands, those instruments of pain and pleasure, returned to her breasts. Instead of touching them as she was certain he'd do, he ran yet more rope under the strands already there. With the new rope now between her breasts, he pulled it so tightly the loops touched. In essence, he'd fashioned a crude bra out of red cord.

"What's changed?" he asked as he tied knots.

Caught. Yours. Submitting to you. "It's tighter. Squishing my breasts."

"Right you are." He flicked her left nipple. "Can you undo my handiwork?"

I don't know if I want to. She tried to shake her upper body. "No."

"But you want to."

"Yes. Of course I do."

"Defiance." He pinched her right nipple. "Oh yes, this is going to be interesting, at least for me. A chance to do what I'm...what I'm good at."

Had that been a moment of hesitancy? Introspection maybe. If so, he wasn't the only one.

"By the time I'm done with you today, you'll have begun a break with the old you. The process won't be complete, far from it, but if you want to say goodbye to the old you, this would be a good time."

Maybe if she thanked him he'd —

No! She wasn't ready for that, yet.

"Before we get down to the business at hand," he said, "I've decided to let you look at yourself."

I already did.

He'd unchained her and guided her back into the small bathroom, via a hold on her arm, before it dawned on her that he wasn't dragging her because she'd willingly matched his steps stride for stride. He positioned her in the dark space then turned on the light.

The first thing she noticed was how limp her hair looked, how haunted her eyes. More than haunted, she acknowledged. There was something else, maybe anticipation.

Could that be?

Yes.

Forcefully dismissing her expression, she turned her attention to her upper body, which was all she could see in the high mirror. The collar was so thick it covered most of her neck, but, fortunately, it wasn't choker-tight. A large, thick ring was embedded in the front. Her elbows stuck out from her sides, her forearms and hands behind her. She just glimpsed the tight, wide leather band around her waist, not that it mattered. Only the red lengths over, under, and between her pinched breasts did. There was something erotic about the way the ropes hugged her flesh. It wasn't enough that the man had captured her, he'd also taken full control of part of what defined her as a woman, a sexual creature.

Earlier, he'd trapped her sex under more proof of his power.

94

This was no simple kidnapping. He'd taken her for one reason—to make her submit to him.

As long as his tools remained on her, she couldn't stop him.

And after?

"Now do you see why I've been calling you a slave?"

It wasn't a question. They both knew the answer.

Why, she longed to ask. Why, she needed to know. But he'd punish her if she asked. Maybe he would anyway.

Risking another look at her expression, she wondered if he could see the anticipation in her eyes. That's what she was seeing, anticipation mixed with dread.

Chapter Seven

"That's enough." He clapped his hands. "You can admire yourself later. Back into the living room."

The cabin looked as if it had been built to survive winter's fiercest storm. She'd be insane to think she could escape the thick log walls or break the thermopane windows.

This amazing, wonderful-smelling place had become her prison.

He stopped near the pack he'd left on the floor, and she resigned herself to joining him there. Maybe it was seeing her image in the mirror, maybe the feel of rope around her breasts was responsible. Whatever the reason, she now thought of herself as a sexual creature. Rope and leather had claimed chunks of her. She'd lost use of her arms and her bare feet wouldn't get her far in the wilderness. With the gag gone, she could call for help that probably wasn't out there.

This nameless man owned her. Possessed every inch of her body.

"Pain, helpless pain is a great motivator for change. It also serves as a pathway into a new existence."

He kept throwing the damnable word 'pain' at her. If she could she'd have torn it apart, smashed it into pieces, burned it.

Maybe.

Her heart hammered as he dug into the bag. She'd resigned herself to accepting what he intended to do, but she couldn't suppress a gasp as he held up a set of silver nipple clamps attached to each other via a slender chain.

Like her fantasies, exactly like the ones her mind had

created.

"I take it you know what these are."

Unable to speak, she nodded.

His expression softened as he ran his fingers over the connecting chain. "This set is the finest money can buy. In fact, I had them created according to my specifications. Once I demonstrated them, most of my co-workers wanted their own pair." Head a little to the side, he held onto one clamp. The rest dangled. "You want to run, right? Throw yourself at the window and take your chances, despite the threat of being cut into pieces." He started the loose end to swaying. "Go on. I'll give you a head start."

Staring at what would soon grab hold of her, she tried to pull her hands free.

"Nah." He shook his head. "That's not going to work. I shouldn't have to point out that I know what I'm doing when it comes to restraining a slave, but I'm wasting my breath." The dangling clamp struck her just above her waist. "I've been in this business long enough to know you'll try to avoid this little decoration. It's instinct."

The hand not holding the clamps snaked out. He took hold of the rope between her breasts and jerked her toward him. She fought to free herself.

"Not going to happen!" He wrenched down and forced her onto her knees.

"Well—" He pulled her back onto her feet. "That was fun, at least it was for me. Nothing's worse than a slave who gives up. Now do you want me to give you a repeat performance or are you going to stand still?"

Stand still? Let him imprison her nipples?

What choice did she have?

She couldn't bring herself to say yes so widened her stance and thrust her breasts at him.

Frowning, he let go of the makeshift bra. "I didn't expect that."

Was he admiring her courage enough to change his mind about hurting her? At least he couldn't know that reality and fantasy were weaving together in her mind. Could he?

Still frowning, he cupped a hand under her right breast and lifted it. Staring unbelieving, she watched as he positioned the open clamp over her nipple and let it close. Pain slammed into her, forcing her to whirl away from him. He yanked her back into place via the red rope and lifted her left breast.

"Stand the fuck still!"

This wasn't happening! It couldn't be —

Once more, metal closed down around a nipple.

"No, no!" Again, she tried to turn her back to him, but his hold on the nipple chain brought her onto her toes, while his renewed grip on her rope bra kept her before him. She threw back her head, her bare feet tattooed the carpet, and she again strained to free her hands.

"Not going to happen, slave. I have you exactly where I want you."

He was right. It didn't matter what she did, or how fiercely she fought him, he'd won this round. Her nipples still ached and burned, but agony was slowly settling into a sensation she now felt mostly in her crotch.

"Let it surround you," her captor muttered. "Lose yourself in the connection between pain and pleasure."

What pleasure? Her whole body was on fire. Even with waves of discomfort radiating throughout her, she forced herself to study what had been done to her. There was something both erotic and beautiful about the sight of silver attached to her breasts. She was particularly drawn to the weight swaying between the clamps. Her breasts had become more, an inescapable connection with her captor. He'd altered them to meet his needs, was altering her so she'd become whatever he wanted her to be.

"Why?" she whispered. "Why?"

"Because I can."

'How long will they remain part of me?' she longed to ask but didn't dare. Maybe the truth was she needed to exist in the moment.

Erotic make-believe had become part of her existence. No longer could she shut off her sexy imaginings so she could function in the day-to-day. Her time of directing an imaginary Master's words and actions had been replaced by a powerful and commanding man.

"Back in the bathroom. Take another look at yourself. Never forget what you see."

Walking without jiggling the clamps was impossible. Still, she shuffled along, staring down at what she could see of herself the whole time. Making it real. Her captor followed with his hand on her shoulder. She was almost comforted by it.

Because he'd left the light on, her image stared back at her the moment she stepped in. This time he joined her, forcing her to press against the sink to accommodate his bulk.

She'd expected what she was seeing, but that didn't make acceptance any easier. Her breasts were barely recognizable. Caught. As helpless as the rest of her. The clamps' weight dragging the twin mounds down.

"Describe what you're seeing and feeling." He punctuated his command by tightening his hold on her shoulder. "Leave nothing out. I'll know if you try."

Of course he would. He'd done the same thing to other women. Wondering how or if they'd survived their time with him, she straightened.

"My breasts are on fire. I feel the…the pain everywhere." Hoping that would satisfy him, she swallowed.

He grabbed her hair and pulled her head back. "That's the surface, slave. Go deeper, damn you."

Don't try to fight him. You can't win. "I can't get used to not having use of my arms. I keep thinking they're free and all I have to do is remember how to work them. The belt — it can be used for so many things. The, um, the same is true of the collar."

He'd slackened his hold on her hair but the potential in his grip coupled with everything else he'd done to her warned her to keep going.

"I feel— I'm acutely aware of the clamps, chain, ropes, leather, and nudity, but a part of me still says this isn't happening. That…"

"That what?"

"I don't know what I was going to say." She couldn't fathom telling her captor about her dream submission. "Everything feels unreal."

"We call that survival instinct." He patted her right cheek. "In time, I'll drive that out of you, which will open you to the depths of your reality. The new you will begin to emerge. You might not recognize that person, but it's necessary. Otherwise, you'd have no value to me."

He was again throwing too much at her. At least, she told herself, he'd forgotten about getting her to expose her emotions to him—or had he?

The body reflected in the mirror didn't belong to her and yet on some dark level it was familiar. She'd been to this place before but only in her mind.

"You're in pain. What other sensations are at play? How about what's going on in your pussy?"

She'd been right. He did understand her on a deep and personal level. Caught between wondering if she dared be honest and needing to keep something, anything to herself, she stared at her reflection. Her nudity and captivity—a lifetime ago she'd fantasized about this happening.

"What did I tell you?" He reached around her and took hold of the chain. "Be honest, damn it."

"I— Please, I don't know how to explain…" The nipple chain was in his grip, her aching breasts at his mercy. "It-it's as if everything I'm experiencing is being played out between my legs. I'm, ah, I'm alive down there."

"It feels good?"

"Good?" she parroted. "I don't know. Different." The instant she'd said the word, she clung to it. "Like nothing I've ever felt."

"That's proof your body is reacting normally."

'How can you say that?' she ached to snap, but she'd do

whatever she had to appease him. To play her role.

"Let's get back to your arms. You won't have use of them back unless it pleases me to do so. How does that make you feel?"

Wanted.

No, not that!

Not long ago he'd been content to hear how much he was hurting her, hadn't he? Why did that have to change?

"Feel? I don't know."

"Yes, you do." He lifted the chain. "You don't want to think about that particular reality, which is exactly why I'm requiring what I am."

The drawing sensation radiating through her breasts and down to her sex emptied her lungs. Trying not to add to what she was being subjected to, she slowly replenished the oxygen in them. His head in the mirror nodded in comprehension of what she'd done. Something about his eyes captured her attention. The Master who'd taken up residence in her imagination had no humanity. He existed as a stick figure she moved around to fit her wishes. In telling contrast, the flesh and blood man beside her was complex. He had a past, a reason for doing what he did.

Maybe she could connect with him.

"This takes me back to something that happened many years ago," she admitted. "It was very different, and yet, in some ways it wasn't."

He looked confused. "Hmm. Interesting. However, I need you to focus on the here and now. Part of what separates humans from animals is our opposable thumbs. Not only has that been taken from you, you in essence don't have arms. What does that mean?"

Damn you for shutting me out! "I can't defend myself."

"Exactly. What else?"

He lowered his hand, bringing her breasts down with it and making her gasp. "What else?" she asked.

"I want you to expand on not being able to defend yourself and while you're doing so, I want you to go back to studying what you see in the mirror."

From the moment he'd grabbed her last night, this man had been part of her every heartbeat. He decided if she could breathe, go to the bathroom, stand or sink to her knees. He was responsible for her lack of clothes, kept her in this claustrophobic space. How could she possibly have thought they might have something in common and all she had to do was find that connection?

"I couldn't stop you from putting those things on me." Shaking anew, she stared at her imprisoned mounds. "And I won't be able to stop you from doing...doing whatever you want to me."

"That's right. I'm in charge."

Hating him for stating the obvious, she forced herself to block out the toilet, sink, and shower. This was all about her, her imprisoned body trapped in a nightmare. Her past didn't matter, and her future was no longer hers to try to map out. Her captor probably didn't care what would happen to the rest of her possessions. He hadn't pressed her about her family, friends, or lovers, which meant they were unimportant to him. He'd wanted a captive, a prisoner, a subject, a slave, and now he had one.

Had her.

No, she forcefully amended as her image blurred. She wasn't his slave. Yet.

"I think you've been at it long enough." He spoke so softly she wasn't certain she'd heard him correctly. "Enforced nudity and bondage are powerful images, but there's only so much a slave-in-training can assimilate at one time."

Her numb breasts screamed back to life when he turned her via the chain. Tears prevented her from seeing clearly, but she understood that he intended to take her out of the bathroom.

It didn't have to be this way. All he had to do was tell her what he wanted and she would have hurried to comply.

Despite her resolve, she whimpered as he hauled her back into the too-masculine living room. Still holding on to the chain, he again reached into the bag and pulled out a digital camera. "I want to share this with someone."

Her breasts throbbed, so she could barely concentrate on what he'd said. Besides, it was unimportant. He'd do whatever he wanted. She couldn't stop him. Another whimper, this one as much from relief as pain escaped once he'd dropped the chain. Leaving her to try to second-guess his next move, he sat in a nearby chair.

"Stand there," he said. He pointed at the floor a few feet in front of him. "The light here isn't perfect, but the flash will make up for it."

In contrast to the tension that threatened to make her muscles cramp, her captor looked completely relaxed, except for how he'd positioned his left leg off to the side, as if he wanted to dismiss its existence.

He turned on the camera and stared at her through the viewfinder. "Turn around. Make it slow."

Someone else was going to see this, maybe more than one person. For all she knew, the shots he was about to take were only the first in an ever-growing collection designed to document her descent into slavery.

Slave? No escape?

"Hey!" he snapped. "Listen, damn it. Turn the fuck around."

AS she clenched her teeth in preparation for obeying, she realized this was the first time he'd sounded truly angry. Even the slightest move sent the damnable chain to swaying. Was it getting heavier? How much discomfort could her poor, trapped breasts stand?

As much as he wanted.

Rotating, despair threatened to overwhelm her. Even without the bathroom mirror, she knew what she looked like—a cruel man's helpless and demeaned captive. Naked and restrained. Willing to grovel at his feet in a desperate attempt to keep from being hurt more.

"Keep your head up. Shoulders back. Face me again. That's right, now spread those legs."

I don't want to do this. You can't make me!

The silent protest didn't help. Between the relentless camera flash, her burning breasts, and uncomfortable arms, she couldn't find the courage to say the words aloud. He'd commanded her to stand with her legs far apart, so that's what she did. So far, she hadn't begged — he hadn't broken her down enough for that.

"You can do better than that, slave." He leaned forward and pointed the camera at her crotch.

No, no, no.

"What's this?" he demanded. "Are you refusing?"

Not trusting what might come out of her mouth, she settled for glaring at him. The camera lens shifted to her face. *Click, click, click*, the flashes practically blinding her. Lost in the cries lodged in her throat, she drew her legs together.

Enough. I've surrendered so much. Leave me with...with something.

"What's that about?" He sounded mildly curious.

She forced herself to face him. "I can't. I won't."

"Can't? Won't? By the time I'm done with you, you'll embrace obedience in ways you never believed possible." He studied her as if she were some specimen that had been presented to him. "Let me guess, you put your parents through hell while you were growing up, always testing the boundaries and breaking them whenever you thought you could get away with it."

She tried to conjure up images of what her parents had looked like but couldn't. They, like everything else before last night, was unimportant. Besides, everything he'd said was wrong.

"You're trying to embarrass me." Even as she said the words, she knew they didn't go far enough. "But I'm not going to play your game."

He put down the camera. "I don't play, ever."

She forced herself to stand in place when he rose then gritted her teeth as he extended both hands toward her breasts. Something in his expression made her wonder if he admired her courage, and she fed off what might've been his newfound respect for her. Then, moving with measured efficiency, he released the tension on the clamps. She shook her breasts free. Renewed blood flowing in her breasts forced out a cry. Trembling, she leaned forward and concentrated on breathing through the pain. The small bit of freedom was wonderful.

"Damn, damn, damn," she muttered.

He grabbed the collar ring and forced her onto her toes. "What was that?" He slapped one breast then the other. She stumbled and swayed. "You were cursing me?"

I don't know.

The measured blows continued. She shook, not just from pain, but the effort to wrench her wrists free. She tried to be quiet but kept making pitiful sounds.

"This is the crux of lesson one," he said conversationally while concentrating on her left breast. "I'll warn you to try not to wear yourself out because it'll take a while. And for the record, I'll win."

Win what? she wanted to know. *And what makes you think I need to be taught something?*

After what seemed forever, the punishment being delivered to her throbbing breast lessened, the time between the blows became longer. Also, he no longer kept her on her toes. Finally, long after she'd forgotten how and why this terrible thing had begun, he seized her shoulders and shoved her ass first into the chair where he'd been sitting. If not for her sweat, she might have slipped off the cool leather and onto the floor. She couldn't think how to straighten, so remained slumped with her hands behind her, her breasts burning, and her legs wide apart.

He took more pictures, most of them of what had to be her wasted face. She could barely see for the hair in her eyes.

"I bore easily," he informed her. "Long as I've been in this business, it takes some doing to keep me entertained and engaged." He started to turn away from her only to stop and clamp his hand over his left thigh. "Damn. God damn."

He wasn't as all-powerful as he wanted her to believe. Somehow, some way, she'd take advantage of that. Maybe.

"All right," he said at length. "As I was saying, I occasionally change things up for entertainment purposes. My entertainment, anyway."

He presented her with his back. Realizing he was returning to the equipment bag, she sat up straight. Much as she wanted to get to her feet she didn't since he hadn't given her permission.

Permission? Had it come to that?

"No," she said at the sight of a long, thin whip. "Oh, no."

"No what? All right, here's the deal. I may alter the punishment part of this lesson if you do exactly as I tell you. For the record, I'm a stern taskmaster." He snapped the whip so it slashed at the air. "I caution you to conduct yourself in such a way that I don't feel it's necessary to demonstrate what I'm capable of. You'll try to do that, won't you?"

What kind of insane question was that? "Yes," she managed.

"Hmm. That isn't a complete response. Rest assured, you'll understand the totality of what's expected of you by the time we're finished, if we ever finish. Now..." He dropped the whip. "Stand up."

I don't know if I can. Much as she longed to throw herself on his mercy, a part of her kept the words locked inside. Maybe they wouldn't do her any good and she'd have demeaned herself for nothing.

Waves of self-loathing passed through her. Her legs had weakened in the short period of time she hadn't been using them.

"Now turn around."

Once she had, he shoved her into the chair. She landed on her knees with her face in the seat. Other than being able to turn her head to the side so she could breathe, she was at his disposal, a fact he drummed into her as he untied her wrists. She didn't know what to think or how to react when he lifted her arms over her head and massaged her shoulders. Bit by bit the strain of her arms' long inactivity was replaced by warmth and lethargy. Maybe she'd been wrong to fear the whip. As long as she did what he wanted, he wouldn't hurt her.

He might even show her kindness.

He brought her arms back down to her sides then slid into a warm and quiet place when he stroked them.

"Back to work," he said and slid two rope strands around her elbows. The rope tightened, forcing her elbows closer together. She groaned and twitched under him as the pressure continued. Her elbows weren't touching, but not much separated them. He knotted the rope then threaded the loose end through the collar at the nape of her neck.

He unfastened the leather around her waist, and she took several deep breaths. It still felt as if she were wearing the too-tight belt.

"That's what I mean by changing things up for my entertainment." He remained so close his thigh pressed against hers—his warm thigh. "Take a moment to assess your new predicament. Then we'll get back to business."

Chapter Eight

Reno debated helping his new slave to her feet, but if he did, she might think he had at least a measure of sympathy for her. Determined not to go down that road until, and unless, he understood himself better, he entertained himself by running the nails of both hands over her sweet, so available buttocks. At first she twitched and tried to move out of his reach, but much sooner than he'd anticipated, she dropped her head and let the chair support her. He hadn't bound her elbows particularly tightly. This new-to-her position left her hands free but useless, which was the point.

At least one point, he amended. Reluctantly taking his leave of her soft buttocks, he pressed a practiced finger against her ass crack.

"Oh," she gasped and lifted her head.

He realized he'd been hoping she'd say more. He wasn't used to quiet slaves. Most of the time, he had to stuff their mouths to keep them from blowing out his eardrums, but even as he'd slapped this slave-in-training's breasts, she'd kept things to almost ladylike gurgles.

"I've called you a slave," he informed her, "but that's a general term. It's time for the specifics, starting with taking another assessment of your receptiveness."

He gave her a few seconds in which to get used to having him at her back door then withdrew the offending digit, reached around her, and touched his forefinger to her mouth.

"Cover it with spit. It goes without saying that if you try to bite me, you'll pay for it. Nod if you understand."

Her head jerked up and down.

"That's a step in the right direction." He worked his finger past her lips and waited for her to part her teeth, which she did. In her mind, she was probably doing what had to be done in an attempt to escape punishment, but willingly giving him access to any part of her body said she'd stopped thinking about herself as existing separately from him.

He pushed in. A fingertip touched the roof of her mouth. She jerked and gagged but didn't try to expel him. Patience hadn't ever been his virtue, but strangely he wasn't in a hurry. In truth, he still wasn't sure why he'd brought her into his world.

As she closed her lips around his finger and started coating it, he allowed himself a small truth. He preferred these moments of artificial intensity to what he had planned for next.

Turning her into something with value in the marketplace via punishment had become a chore.

"That's it." He encouraged her efforts by patting her ass. "Get every inch wet so it'll go in easier."

She stiffened.

"I can't have said something you hadn't already figured out. Damn it, I know you're smart enough to have put one and one together."

A ragged sigh escaped her, and after a telling pause, she went back to bathing his finger. Moments like this with a slave had always been a turn-on. He hadn't concerned himself with the specifics of why seeing a slave surrender to the inevitable gave him so much pleasure, just knew that it did.

Today he wasn't so sure.

Damn it, facing his mortality had really messed him up, kept him from the action so long he'd lost his edge.

His passion for the job.

The hell it had!

Fighting thoughts that had stalked him since he'd nearly

died, he pulled out and repositioned himself in preparation for another kind of invasion. The chair was so low he'd be hard pressed to get the alignment right, but the last thing he'd do was kneel behind her. He was her superior, her Master. A man with a bad leg.

The instant he knocked at her rear door, she bowed her back so her ass dropped a few inches.

"What the hell are you doing, slave?" He slapped her ass. "Get your bung hole up here."

"Why?" she muttered and pressed her forehead to the chair seat. Her buttocks rose as if in invitation. He knew that wasn't the case, at least not now. If he kept after her, the time would come when she'd beg for things she couldn't comprehend today.

That's what today was for, starting to change her, turning her into a sex-hungry slut.

His.

"Why?" he parroted. He positioned his slick finger over the puckered opening and pushed in. "Because I can."

Her muscles were trying to expel him, but he'd had his finger squeezed enough times that the tightness didn't surprise him. Eventually, once he'd trained her, he'd fuck her back there, but he saw no reason to risk injury to his cock while she was this raw.

Besides, truth was, the damn accident had put his libido on the back burner.

Time to reverse that, starting with climbing back on the slave-training saddle. No longer asking himself what the hell his life was about or mucking around in the hell-hole that was his past.

Adding action to anticipation, he continued the invasion. Her legs jumped and twitched and she breathed as if she were running. He let her turn her head this way and that, figuring she wasn't getting enough of a look to satisfy her curiosity. Knowing she was trying to keep her ass where he wanted it distracted him from the task at hand. In short, her reaction had come to mean more than his.

"This belongs to me." He shoved, concentrating on keeping the alignment right as he did. "If I want to plug you, you'll be plugged." He withdrew a little, pleased by how her anal muscles now struggled to keep him in her. "If I decide to fuck you there, you'll pull your ass cheeks apart to help accommodate me, got it?"

He'd just hit her with a particularly demeaning comment so wasn't surprised by her lack of a response. Curious to see what it would take to break through her emotional barriers, he again changed position and finger-fucked her in earnest. His back protested his position and the harsh movements. More frustrating, his overworked leg howled every time he tried to rest his weight on it.

So, if he couldn't spend much time hammering at this particular part of today's lesson, at least he'd make the best of the moments he had.

"This is what it's going to feel like as you're being ass-fucked." He plundered and retreated, dove deep, followed by protracted withdrawal. "I'm only using one finger, so unless you've done this a lot, taking my cock will make you feel as if you're being ripped apart."

"Oh, oh, oh."

Beautiful sounds, ones he'd nearly forgotten during the months of hell.

Relishing her rapid-fire grunts, he ignored the burning sensations running up his arm. He was strong again, no longer a damn nearly dying weakling. This was what he excelled at, what built him up, while at the same time taught his subjects the meaning of surrender.

As she bent her knees, he figured she was trying to find a more comfortable position. Taking advantage of her distraction, he hooked his finger and lifted. She immediately relocked her legs.

"Keep your asshole where I can use it."

Judging by how much her legs now shook, he had no doubt she was on emotional overload. Perfect timing for kicking things up another notch.

He pressed his foot against the inside of one ankle then the other in a silent command for her to spread her legs. Letting loose with something between a grunt and a whimper, she complied. He gave her time to get used to the altered strain before redoubling his attack. His forefinger was going numb, and he guessed his hand would soon cramp. The self-inflicted burn marched up his arm.

She now grunted with every breath she took and no longer tried to lift her head. Her useless fingers kept curling into fists. He was back in familiar territory, doing what he'd been doing since a man had taken a scared and homeless boy under his wing and into a world of domination and surrender.

Intuition and experience told him she'd lost all control over her responses so he slipped his free hand between her legs and aimed for her pussy. Sex fluids didn't quite pour from her, but she was a long way from dry. He could have pointed her condition out to her but decided to leave that for later in the game. Today, he'd simply press his point. Maybe emotionally tear her apart.

I'm a damn bastard.

Wishing he could see her expression, he tried to take hold of her labial lips, but the swollen flesh was too slippery. He compensated by ramming two soaked fingers into her sex hole. Bent nearly in half the way he was, his back and leg kicked up their complaints.

"Get that ass of yours up here, slave."

You don't have to do this.

She lifted herself onto her toes and managed to stay in position long enough for him to pump both of her holes. As she slumped back onto the balls of her feet, he yanked out of her tight rear passage and whacked her buttocks.

"What'd I tell you? You were supposed to stay in position."

"I'm sorry," she muttered into the chair.

Her choked tone made him wonder if he'd taken her too far, and reminded him of the danger in losing self-control.

The years of anger and need for revenge were behind him, damn it! He was no longer the crazy, lost teenager he'd once been.

Then what am I?

He placed the finger that had been in her bung against her left palm. She closed her hand around it, giving him proof that the elbows' tie hadn't cut off her circulation.

"What are you sorry about?" It took some doing, but he managed to continue fucking her pussy. "Go on, damn it. Finish what you started to say."

"I-I don't know what you want."

There was the strangled tone every Carnal trainer knew and exploited. Her drenched pussy said more than a million words could.

"Right now, what I want isn't the point." He switched to a seductive tone. "I'm creating new needs in you. You won't know what to do with them, let alone how to handle them." She didn't respond so he slowed the thrusting action. "You feel as if you're drowning in sensation, don't you?"

"Yes," she whispered.

That might be the most honest thing she'd said since he'd grabbed her. Curious to see how much more he could get her to reveal, he withdrew and fingered her hard, hot clit. "You need to climax." He touched her sex trigger again, then abandoned it. "Nothing comes close to being as important as getting off. You'd give up food in exchange for a climax. Even water has become a poor second."

Do I really want to do this?

She turned her head, giving him a glimpse of her tears. The unexpected sight distracted him, touched a place he didn't want touched.

"What is it?" he asked.

The way her sigh lasted, he knew she was trying to keep her emotions from him. He wasn't sure whether either of them could. "I don't understand myself." Her trembling slowed. "I'm afraid of you, and yet you're familiar. Someone..."

Taken aback by her comment, he planted both hands on her buttocks. Her sigh ended in a whimper.

"I wish I hadn't said... I don't know why I did."

Was she trying to forge a connection between them, giving him a small piece of herself so maybe he'd do the same in turn? Other slaves had tried that tactic, but only when he was hurting them, not in moments of relative peace.

Who are you, slave?

Trying to shake off the unexpected question, he massaged her shoulders. "Let me take a guess. Your sexual fantasies include men like me, don't they?"

Her silence told him more than any words could. His job called for transforming women into what their owners wanted, not tapping into females' submissive natures. Truth was, he never concerned himself with whether a particular slave embraced or fought the loss of self-determination. He knew how to get to the desired end result, discussion over.

Yesterday, he'd taken one look at her and had known she wanted a man capable of making her crawl and loving the act. What he hadn't figured on was how he'd react.

"Straighten," he ordered.

Watching her strain as she lifted her breasts off the chair distracted him from heavy thoughts, so he nearly pushed her back down so he could again focus on the effort but he'd put off the second part of what this lesson was about long enough.

Time to teach her the depth and width of pain.

Time to do what he knew how to.

No longer alone.

Still on her knees, Kaci tried to make use of her arms. She could move them, after a fashion. They felt as if they belonged to someone else, and yet she'd have to get them to obey in order to have a chance at getting free.

Free? The word was as foreign as the world she now lived in.

"To state the obvious, they're pretty useless," he pointed

out. "I take it that isn't something you've ever experienced."

"No, never. Imagined it a few times but— Why did you—?"

"Come up with that particular restraint? Sometimes I want to keep a tie as simple as possible. Now stand."

Her body hummed with pent-up desire as she struggled to do as he'd commanded. She'd fought the sexual tide but he'd taken her to a place where a climax had been only a breath away. However, he'd stopped stimulating her. Not long ago, only her restraints had kept her with him. Now she wanted—no, surely not the man!

Shutting down the thought, she redoubled her efforts. She tried not to acknowledge his steady gaze while awkwardly getting her feet under her.

"The leg with the rope on it," he said, "put your foot on the chair."

Complying took several attempts, but she finally achieved the nearly impossible. He untied the ankle rope. He even helped her lower her leg once he was done. She looked at him.

The lines around his mouth were as prominent as the last time she'd taken note of them, and he was definitely favoring his left leg. She stopped caring when he picked up his camera and began taking more pictures.

"Who are you sending these to?" she risked asking.

He frowned. "A friend, someone who'll appreciate them for what they are."

The way he said 'friend' distracted her from the relentless clicking. She could've been wrong, but it sounded as if he seldom used the word. If he was part of some kinky sex club, how did the various members refer to each other?

Against her better judgment, she looked down at herself. Her roped breasts were swollen, her nipples still red from the clamps.

"Will they show up on the Internet?"

"I haven't decided."

He was probably saying that as a way of messing with her mind. Standing there, she wondered what he'd think if she told him about her fantasies. Would he use them to his advantage or — how could she even think this? — would he take what she told him to turn their time together into incredible reality?

Shocked that she'd entertained the possibility, she shook her head in an effort to stop it. Being his captive had given rise to the question, that's all. She'd never want to be his slave.

Slave. Owned. Desired.

Unexpected movement from him pulled her from the crazy thought. He'd put down the camera and was picking up the whip.

"No," she gasped as she back-peddled. "Please, no."

He blinked, stared at the whip, frowned.

"You don't tell me what I can or can't do. No one does." He snapped the air with the thin length. "I'm going to educate you, transform you into something useful to me. You might think that being stripped of your clothes and restrained is lesson enough, but you're still the old you. It's time to become something new. Mine."

He'd thrown his domineering words at her before, but that didn't make it any easier this time. Sweat again drenched her. At the same time, she was cold.

And still hot.

'I don't want to become yours,' she longed to tell him, but it wouldn't do any good. He wouldn't listen.

He'd kept on snapping the whip while talking.

"This is about relating to your body in a new way, of getting deeper into yourself than you believed possible."

There was something seductive about what he was offering. She dreaded being whipped. At the same time, she couldn't help but embrace his words.

"Pain seduces. It takes the receiver into a new world, one she can't emotionally distance herself from — or want to."

Was that possible? Could pain seduce? Desperate to believe him as a way of dealing with her dread, she studied his arm. He worked the whip as if it were an extension of him, an exquisite tool.

"Take what I offer, slave. That's all you have to do today."

He fastened his gaze on her left flank. An instant later, a sharp stinging sensation there rocked her.

"No! Oh, please, don't."

He again whipped her in the same place. A second wave of pain bled into the first. He lifted his arm for another blow, but she ran past him, heading for the door. Half-facing him as he slowly ate up the distance between them, she backed up to the door and gripped the knob.

The whip landed on her belly.

"Please, oh, God, please."

"There is no god here, never forget that."

His voice was so calm, a whisper of sanity in a world being defined by pain. He'd locked the door, but she kept wrestling with it while he planted blow after blow. She twisted, but he accomplished his goal. The whip didn't cut her flesh, not that it made a difference. It was as if she were being stung by countless wasps.

Screaming, she pushed away from the damn worthless door and ran back the way she'd come. Maybe her intention had been to try to escape into the kitchen, maybe she hadn't had any plan. Whatever the answer, she never got a chance to see if another room was any safer because he grabbed the rope between her elbows and yanked.

"You aren't going anywhere, slave. That's not how it works."

Fire bloomed on her buttocks. Fighting a scream, she stood shaking in the middle of the masculine room with her back to her captor. She wouldn't, couldn't face him. Didn't want to see his expression.

He whipped her repeatedly, the blows landing on her ass cheeks. They caught fire, taking her back to all those times her old man had spanked her. Sometimes she'd known why she was being punished. Mostly, though, the bastard had done so because he was mad at the world.

She'd learned to take her childhood punishment in

silence. The less she reacted, the sooner he quit. If it were possible, she'd do the same today.

"I don't believe in deep distress," her captor told her as she quivered before him. "There have been a few times I forgot my creed and— Tell me how much this hurts."

She tried to hold her ground, but the distress he'd mentioned made her feet dance. Her constrained breasts pulsed. Every time the whip landed on an ass cheek, she was compelled to turn it from him with the result that the next blow abraded her other buttock. The sensations built up inside her, an accumulation of the unwanted—his way of demonstrating his mastery over her.

Too much!

Howling more from outrage than pain, she broke rank and again ran. This time she circled the room's perimeter, dodging furniture. His features grim, he kept after her.

"You're not going to get away, there's nowhere for you to go. No way you can free your elbows or breasts. The sooner you accept the inevitable—"

"Go to hell!"

Had she really said that? Certain that she'd enraged him, she looked back at him. His jaw remained set, but what unnerved her the most was how his eyes glittered. He was enjoying this.

Of course he was, she acknowledged while putting all her energy into keeping ahead of him. No one would do something so incomprehensible unless he loved dominating.

Domination. Restraining and stripping her because he could.

She'd circled the room for the third time before she realized what he was doing. He wasn't really pursuing her. Instead, he snapped the whip behind her. Other than slowly turning, he wasn't putting out any effort. In contrast, she was wearing herself out, still dancing to his tune.

There was no escape from this room. She might bolt into the kitchen, but if he didn't want her in there, he'd simply haul her out and back into here. Then his diabolical game would begin again.

Somewhere between resigned and determined to hold on to a shred of dignity, she jammed her toes into the carpet and stopped with her side to him.

"Do what you're going to. I can't stop you."

"You could try."

"Why? So you can get off watching me?"

A pause. "Not just that. I want to see even more fire from you."

One second they were carrying on an insane conversation, the next the whip struck the side of her breast. Again, driven by instinct, she hunched her shoulders the little the elbows' tie allowed and presented him with her back.

The next blow laid a hot line on her thigh.

"Ah!"

"There's the sound I need to hear. Let's see what it takes to get that out of you again."

Don't move! Don't run like some blind panicked beast!

Ruled by the command coming from a place she didn't know existed in her, she held her head high. The whip kissed and teased, sometimes landing hard enough to force out another cry. She didn't try to keep track of where the strikes landed, and when he ordered her to turn in circles, she gave in to the harsh words.

The two of them were in a room built of wood, heated by wood, illuminated by the sun. No one heard her and no one saw him aim and aim and aim at her naked, defenseless body. She thought of herself as a ballerina twirling on top of a music box, only there was no music here, only whip snaps and the sounds he forced from her.

Her fingers kept reaching for something they couldn't reach; her breasts throbbed, her hair was plastered to her neck and cheeks, and her body — her hurting, on-fire body existed as something separate from her mind.

"Stay with the sensations. Take them as far into you as they'll go. Surrender your breasts, buttocks, and thighs to the throbbing."

119

"I can't... I don't..."

"Don't try to speak." A spark struck the top of one breast then the other. "Words require too much concentration." The whip laid down a burning line on the inside of her right thigh. "Feel your body. Listen to everything it's telling you. Become primitive for it, and for me."

He wanted her to do something for him? She would, she would if only he'd stop hurting her.

"You're still thinking." He sounded disappointed. "Sensation is the only thing you should care about." Fire briefly danced over her belly. "I wasn't going to do this so soon but I've decided to take advantage of where I've sent you today."

Once again, he was giving her too much to think about. Something hot enveloped her. Now that he'd stopped switching her, she fought to comprehend where the heat was coming from. Some of it, of course, was the result of her beating, but that wasn't all. She was exhausted, engulfed.

Engulfed in what? Sensation? He'd kept using that word.

"Stand by my equipment bag," he said in a conversational tone. "You will do that for me, won't you? I won't have to do anything to make it clear that this is an order."

His words were such a salve to her wounded psyche that she was standing near the bag before the ramifications sank in. The lump on the floor was where he kept his — his slave tools.

"Go on. Take a look."

Trembling, so she had to widen her stance to keep from falling, she watched him upend it and shake out its contents. She couldn't get past the reality that she was closer to him than she'd been since he'd stopped her from running into the kitchen.

"There." He picked up a pair of handcuffs. "That's one of the things I'm after."

"Cuffs? But—"

"Your shoulders and arms have been under that particular strain long enough. Time to change things around."

What an idiot she was, she acknowledged as he stepped behind her. She cursed her blind capitulation when he snapped the cuffs over her wrists and released her elbows, but what could she do? He'd overwhelm her if she resisted.

She was still trying to make her peace with the freedom to her elbows and the harsh metal around her wrists as he slid heated fingers over her arms. She couldn't relax.

"In time," he said, "you'll welcome my touch. The journey has already begun. Eventually, you'll turn yourself completely over to me."

"No."

She tried to step away from him. A masculine arm snaked around her throat and he pulled her back against his hard body. He fingered her right breast. "I've always enjoyed having a slave struggle, but you need to learn it won't do you any good." He spoke into her ear. "You're mine. Mine. End of discussion."

Chapter Nine

'Mine.' Kaci could barely think for the words he'd just whispered. She'd been helpless from the first moment he'd touched her, but the totality of her situation hadn't truly sunken in before. She had no choice but to allow him to support her weight. Thanks to him, her body bore countless whip marks. He wasn't done punishing her.

Moving in slow-motion, he reached around her torso with his free arm and lightly rubbed her right nipple.

"Tell me you hate being touched like this. Say something to make me believe you loathe everything about what has happened to you."

The necessary words backed up in her throat, but she couldn't get them out. Every muscle and nerve felt acutely alive. Her entire system was ragged, out of its element and trying to make sense of this new existence he'd thrust her into. The longer he massaged her nipple, the less anything except the erotic manipulation registered.

"It isn't as bad as you need it to be, is it?" He switched to her other nipple, his fingers kissing her tight flesh. "One minute I'm subjecting you to pain, the next there's pleasure."

"No," she whispered. "I don't want—"

"Maybe your mind doesn't yet, but your body is primitive. It understands pleasure and pain, fullness and hunger, warmth and cold. After it has been satisfied, it cares about nothing else. You have potential, slave. Potential I will exploit."

This man who'd taken her from what she was familiar with could've been a poet. He used words in ways she'd never experienced.

"In many respects," he continued in his sing-song tone, "the first days are the hardest. Resistance comes from many sources, fear high among them. Slaves want back the world they understand. The future is beyond their comprehension because the present is so intense."

Keep rubbing my nipple, please. Hold me against you so I can feel your heat. Give me some of your strength. Make me believe you're doing this because down deep you care for me.

"As for why we make the initial impact so intense — otherwise the transformation takes much longer, wasting valuable time that could be put to better use."

She was a prisoner in this man's world. Sooner or later he'd rape her — wasn't that why he'd taken her? — but he wanted more from her.

He wanted everything.

"Seeing you helpless turns me on, satisfies a need, but I promised you a measure of relief. It's time you got it."

He stood her upright. She concentrated on trying to control her shaking as he slowly unwound the red lengths from around her breasts. The restored blood flow burned through her. She hoped he'd massage her, but he picked up something she couldn't see with her back to him. Whatever it was, it felt soft along her spine.

Suddenly, he grabbed her hair and yanked, making her stare at the ceiling. An instant later, something covered her eyes. Panicked, she tried to shake it off.

"Don't!" he snapped. "Damn it, you know better."

I can't help it.

"This is called sensory deprivation," he said once he'd fastened the blindfold around her head. He patted her cheeks. "It's an extremely effective method of encouraging a subject to focus on what a Master wants her to."

Master? Had he used that word before? Maybe it had only been part of her fantasies.

He spun her in a half-circle, and she assumed she was facing him. Darkness conspired with her useless arms to threaten to push her into madness. She wasn't sure she could stay in control.

Seconds passed. He wasn't touching her so she had no way of knowing whether he was where he'd been. For all she knew, he could have left the room. Maybe he was sitting in one of the chairs watching her, waiting for her to fall apart.

Where are you? Please don't leave me.

No, damn it, she wouldn't beg! Pride was all she had left.

Being deprived of the ability to see made her less sure of her balance and she, again, widened her stance. What a sight she must be for a man who considered himself a master of human flesh.

The passing seconds were like never-ending fingernails on a blackboard. Locked within herself, she became even more aware of the metal around her wrists and the collar hugging her neck. She didn't know what to call the sensations on and around her breasts, just that they were an accumulation of everything they'd been subjected to. He obviously was a master of abuse — and of stimulation.

Small fires continued to burn throughout her body. The way the countless tiny sparks heated and caressed her flesh, she wasn't sure she wanted them to end. Sticky juices clung to her pussy and the insides of her thighs. Just thinking about what he'd done to her sex and ass hole started a new flood.

Not aroused! No, damn it, not imprisoned by sexual need. Yet.

"You're a work of art, an erotic sculpture. In time you'll fully embrace your sexuality, slave."

Startled by his unexpected voice, she tried to determine where it was coming from. She had little enough left, just a small measure of pride. If he thought she'd bow before him, he was mistaken.

"Your body has pretty much taken everything it's capable of today. You're still high on adrenaline and stimulation, but there's going to be a crash. You'd love to have something to eat and drink followed by a shower and sleep, wouldn't you?"

Sleep? Yes! Oblivion.

"You're more vulnerable than you ever thought it was possible to be. Any minute now, your body will say enough. It can't take any more. But it'll have to."

In her mind's eye, he was reclining in one of the leather chairs. She imagined he was sipping a drink. Maybe he'd stripped off his clothes in preparation for forcing himself on her. His blood-engorged cock would stand out from his lean yet muscled body and he'd idly massage it.

What hole would he push it into?

Shuddering, she clamped her mouth shut. She'd tried giving oral sex after she'd been drinking but hadn't gotten anything out of the effort beyond a sore jaw and a feeling of yuck. Of course, if she were forced —

"You're going to call me Master. I don't need to spell out what will happen if you don't do as I command."

Master. Like in her fantasy.

Both recoiling from and embracing the comparisons, she squared her shoulders and lifted her head, only to regret the action. All she'd really done was draw his attention to her breasts.

"Someone your age has probably had a few hard knocks, relationships that went sour. Maybe you've been raped."

Try as she did not to react, undoubtedly he'd noticed her tension. Fortunately, he had no way of knowing she'd learned the meaning of the word thanks to her father's drunken attempts.

"That's what I thought." He sounded sympathetic. "You got in over your head a few times, right?"

"Right." *You have no idea.*

"What did that teach you?"

To hell with trying to placate him. He was getting what he wanted. "Not to trust men. Or anyone."

He didn't immediately reply, making her wonder what he intended to do with that piece of information.

"Did you ever trust?"

"Go to hell." *Don't say that again. He'll punish you.*

"Hit a nerve, did I? For the record, slave, eventually you'll tell me. There isn't anything you can keep from me. Would you like to know why?"

She should ignore him and march—march where? Do what blind and without use of her hands?

"Because I'm becoming your Master."

"No you aren't. No one's ever going to control me again." *No! I didn't say that!*

Once again, silence stretched out. Then, "Again? You have a hell of a lot of old tapes playing inside you, slave. Of course, you don't want to share them. But you will."

"No," she moaned. Then, hating her cowed tone, she lifted her head. "Is that what it takes for you to feel like a man? The only way you can get it up is to force a woman to submit?"

"Careful. You're in dangerous territory."

She didn't need his warning. If she could've taken back her words, would she have? She didn't know. The only thing she was certain of was that she'd never been more alive. Her childhood and time behind bars as a teenager had tested her courage. Those things had only been a prelude to today.

With her Master.

Master.

* * * *

Kaci hadn't fought when her captor—not Master—had taken hold of the collar's ring. Hard as she'd tried to convince herself that she'd only stumbled after him because resistance would have been futile, something else had been at play. Against all reason, she'd wanted to see what he had in mind.

How he intended to force that one word from her.

She'd nearly panicked as he'd backed her to a chair and

tied her ankles to the front chair legs so they were apart and her pussy exposed. Then he'd pushed on her chest, knocking her off balance. The seat was so deep she'd wound up leaning back, with her upper body supported by her tailbone and shoulders. At least, she tried to comfort herself, she wasn't sitting on her shackled hands because she'd pulled them up against her waist.

What did her hands, shoulders, or spine matter? Her pussy was available to him.

"That was ridiculously easy," he said. "How does this make you feel?"

Exposed. Vulnerable. "You know."

"Yes, I do. As soon as I'm done taking more pictures, we'll get to why I chose this position."

I already know.

Even with her heart's furious beating, she heard the faint sounds she had no choice but to get used to. Imagining the lens close to her exposed pussy made her blush, and yet, she couldn't help but wonder how whoever received the shots would respond. She'd lost control over her world, but maybe she could bring a man or men to their own edges.

Maybe Master was at his brink.

Shocked at the realization that she'd thought of this dominating stranger as Master, she tried to bring her knees together. "Not going to happen, slave. However, you have brought up something I should have thought of."

She heard rustling sounds. All too soon he wrapped rope around her left knee. "Don't," she muttered. "Oh, damn, don't."

He didn't say anything, only ran another loop over her knee and pulled on the rope, forcing that leg far out to the side. He tapped the inside of her thigh. "Go on, try to move."

She couldn't, of course. He switched to her other side, and she tried to ignore what he was doing. Then he drew her right leg outward, making her fight to sit up.

"That's good to see." He jerked on the strands. "I didn't

think I'd pushed all the fight out of you yet, but every slave's different."

Why had she wasted what little energy she'd still had? It hadn't taken him any time at all to immobilize her legs. Feeling alive in ways that both alarmed and intrigued her, she gave up and sagged back again.

Owned. Controlled.

Undoubtedly he was studying his handiwork, maybe playing with himself while looking at her exposed sex.

"Your pussy is both your undoing and your greatest strength." Like too many times before, his words rolled over her like a warm wave. "In time, you'll crave my every touch there. Think about it. No more worrying about how to pay the bills. Everything will revolve around waiting for me to grant you pleasure, pleasure that will bleed into the pain and become one."

He'd said something like that before. Before she'd been too overwhelmed to try to analyze what he'd been spelling out, but—and maybe it was being blinded—now his words became vital. One thing she was sure of, he was talking about something that would take place over a long period of time.

'I can't do this,' she ached to tell him. *'Kill me now. Don't draw it out.'*

"You don't shave your pussy. There isn't much down there so—maybe I'll leave it like that for a while. Let you wonder when I'll get out a razor, hope I know what I'm doing."

No!

"Pain first. Taking you to that place where only trying to escape registers. Experiencing the ultimate in helplessness."

No, no, no!

"You're quiet." Something made a slapping sound. "I don't think I've ever had a slave like you."

She didn't dare think about the women—not slaves— who'd come before her. Knew only that what she didn't want was about to happen.

Did she?

Something landed on her right breast near her armpit. At first, she thought he'd struck her with the palm of his hand, but whatever this was felt flat. Alert and confused, she swung her upper body away. A moment later, the same thing hit her left breast. This blow was harder than the first, and stung. She'd spent too much energy trying to convince herself that not being able to see wasn't that bad, that she preferred not having to analyze his expression. But that was before he'd twice hit her with something she couldn't identify.

Right breast again, followed by the left. Making her jerk one direction and the other, compelling her to shrink away, even though she wound up smashing her hands. The blows were getting stronger, the aftermath lasting. Was that rubber, some kind of devilish swatter?

"These are my breasts, mine to use, abuse, or reward as I see fit. You're turning them over to me whether you want to or not, losing control, becoming mine."

If there was a rhythm to the blows, she couldn't find it. The swatter struck every part of her wildly jiggling breasts. Heat hummed through them, pain vibrating and never ending. She kept thinking he'd get bored focusing on that one part of her body and would start on her pussy. The longer he assaulted her, the more convinced she became that he was tireless.

He'd whip her until...

Whip? Not that, really, and not pain so much as too much sensation, knowing he was in charge, helplessness clawing into what remained of her. She rolled left and right, left and right, surged upright only to collapse, strained against the damnable ropes around her knees and ankles, the cuffs, fought to see past the blindfold.

Would he ever let her see again?

"Can't, can't...please, I can't..."

"I know this is hard, but it must be done. Otherwise, you'll be incomplete. Unfulfilled. Useless."

Those words made even less sense than other things he'd said. She might have told him so if heat wasn't spreading around to her back and licking down her spine. More fire played over her belly, heading closer and closer to her mons, whispering warnings and promises to her pussy.

Done in and fascinated by the change, she stopped trying to escape the swatter.

"You're tipping over the edge, taking vital steps toward sexual slavery, but there's only one way you'll reach the goal. By my hand."

Sweat seeped under the blindfold and stung her eyes. She licked spittle from the corners of her mouth but couldn't do anything about what dripped off her chin. More sweat stuck her to the seat.

She tensed the instant he placed something on her left thigh. Then her exhausted body sagged. Her throbbing breasts continued to exist as something more than the rest of her. It took her a while to realize he'd stopped attacking them and must have put down the swatter.

"Intense. Almost more than your nervous system can handle. For the record, we aren't done by half."

"I...can't..."

"Ah, but you have to."

As soon as she heard the buzzing sound, she knew he'd turned on a vibrator. Her sex fluttered in anticipation. Hopefully, this was the start of the pleasure he'd told her about. If it took calling him Master to get him to place it against her, she'd do so. She wouldn't mean it of course — of course — but he didn't need to know.

A sensation similar to what had gotten her through many solitary nights swept over her, except this was stronger than the battery-driven toys she was accustomed to. The vibration hadn't lasted long enough, barely alerted her to the possibilities. Desperate for more, she lifted her buttocks off the chair.

He chuckled. "That's what I thought. You're a horny little slave. Ready for another sample, are you?"

She'd just opened her mouth to answer in the affirmative when he again touched his tool to her labia. Like before, the contact didn't last long enough. "What is it? It...it won't hurt me, will it?"

"If you're asking if I intend to shock your pussy, the answer is no. This is a supercharged vibrator I helped design."

What did he mean by supercharged? What was it capable of?

Another press of hard, vibrating rubber to her defenseless core made her jump and whine. Instead of torturing her via the briefest taste of its potential like before, he held his creation against her. Sexual wave after sexual wave slammed into her. Overloaded, she tried to scoot away, but, of course, he'd made that impossible.

"What are you—you can't—oh, please!" She squirmed and bucked.

"Just waiting for you to answer my question, slave. Do you know what a pussy vibrator is?"

Powerful. Relentless. More than I can handle. "Yes, of course!"

He had no pity in him. Even though she squirmed and begged, he kept the over-muscled tool on her.

"Tell me the truth, slave. Has a man ever done this to you? Maybe this is how you bring yourself off. The stronger, the better."

Answer him. Anything to make him stop. "No. I wouldn't—oh, please."

"Then you play with yourself."

"Not...not with that. Oh, God!" She couldn't stop bucking. Knowing she was trapped made it even worse. And better. "I never—"

As suddenly as the erotic torture had begun, it stopped. In the aftermath of the intimate assault, she sagged like a punctured balloon. Her legs shook and cramped, and yet she needed him to touch her again.

"Did you climax?"

"What? No." *Maybe. It's all too much.*

"But you wish you had. It would make things easier."

It didn't sound like a question, so she made no attempt to answer. She couldn't remember where she'd first heard the phrase 'rag doll', but that was exactly how she felt. The only difference was that part of her remained on high alert.

He wasn't done with her. Far from it.

"Long as I've been doing this," he said, "I occasionally wondered why I hadn't burned out. After my accident, whether I worked with another slave was unimportant. That, in a large part, is why I took you."

She was some kind of experiment? "Why do you do what you do? You could get help, stop being cruel." Fearing his reaction, she cringed.

"Cruel? Give me a little more time with you and you won't be calling it that."

It was only her desperate attempt to humanize him in her mind that had her half believing he was making her a promise. He'd turned her on—or maybe the truth was his earlier manipulation of her body had started her down that road. Maybe—oh, what was she thinking? It was all too much, a thousand times worse than being behind bars had been.

"Your sexual nature is your ultimate weakness and my strength," he said. "My prize. That's what you're going to become, my bounty, my possession."

Much as she longed to scream at him, she stared up at the man she couldn't see. Between her too-sensitive breasts and the fiery need humming through her pussy, she no longer cared that she was naked. He'd taken her down to basics and intended to keep her there for as long as it entertained him to do so. The sooner she accepted her lot the sooner— what?

What was it he'd just said, that he intended to turn her into his possession.

His piece of flesh.

Master.

The humming she both dreaded and anticipated

began again. Ignoring her spent body, she tightened her muscles. Her sex remained open to him. It had become his playground.

There. Another touch, a whisper of contact.

"Hmm."

"Like that, don't you. What you'd like even more is to climax, but you have to earn the right."

Damn him for confusing her!

The too-powerful vibrator slid over her aching labia. An instant later the sensation ended.

Please. Help me –

"I'm going to ask you some questions," he said, "and you're going to answer. My reaction to those answers will determine the course of the rest of this lesson."

Another touch, even shorter than the last, the barest touch. Groaning in need, she arched toward him.

"You lack ambition. If you had career plans, you wouldn't have been doing what you were. You'd have a job that'd last more than a few months, a decent place to live. Don't you care what's going to happen to you come winter?"

"I-I'll find something. I always do."

"Not good enough." The vibrator settled against her opening. Power blasted through her.

"What – oh please – what do you want?"

By way of answer, if that's what it was, he subjected her to a series of touches and losses that had her completely off balance. Despite her vow not to respond, she yelped each time the fast-moving rubber came into contact with her pussy. Sometimes his weapon attacked her clit, other times he focused on her labia, but in the end, it was all the same – too much.

Not long enough.

He kept asking questions designed to strip her. Where were her parents? Why didn't she have a permanent home? Why hadn't she settled on a career? What had ended her romantic relationships? Could she name a single close female friend? At first she evaded and dodged, but he kept after her until she had no choice but to give him what he wanted. He wouldn't let her climax. He knew how to keep her teetering on the brink and incapable of anything except the truth.

"I'm not in touch with my parents. They want nothing to do with me. I don't need them. I live, that's all, one day at a time. Seeing different parts of the country, feeling the wind, sun, and rain on my skin. Being free."

"Why is freedom so important?"

"It is. Damn it, it is!" *Except when I let my imagination loose.*

"Why?"

The question was gentle and, at that moment, her pussy wasn't under attack. Her head had been sagging but now she lifted it, again strained to see him.

"I've been locked up."

"By who?"

"The law."

"How old were you?"

Too late to stop. She had to finish what she'd begun or he'd make her pay for it. "Sixteen at the beginning. Eighteen before they let me go."

The buzzing that had become the center of her existence quieted. After a few seconds she realized she was listening to the sound of both of them breathing. She didn't understand any of this.

"What did you do?" He touched her cheek. "Never mind. You can tell me later."

"I don't want to."

"I know you don't, but you have to."

Something had changed about his tone. Whatever it was, it went with his fingers on her cheek. Moments later, he untied her legs. As grateful as she was to be able to bring them together, she had to clench her teeth to keep from begging him to let her come.

He removed her blindfold. She blinked repeatedly but couldn't bring him into focus. Her eyes burned, yet she didn't believe she'd cried. Most likely sweat was responsible.

Touch me down there. That's all it'll take, a single touch.

"I'm giving you a choice," he said. "If you want, I'll take you right to the shower, followed by giving you something to eat." He stared at her pussy. "Or you can start with another kind of relief."

Looking at the tool, now on the chair arm, was easier than meeting his eyes. The silver and red vibrator appeared so innocent sitting there. Just closing her legs had given her back a small amount of privacy, a mute statement about the need for self-determination.

Shaking her head, she opened herself to him. "I hate you," she muttered.

"Yeah, I know."

He picked up the vibrator and turned it on. The way the head shimmied made her think of a rattlesnake about to strike.

"Just do it. Get it over with."

Not pointing out that she was in no position to order him to do anything, he reached into the space she'd provided and separated her labial lips. His fingers were so gentle, a stark contrast to the tool he'd used to tear her into pieces.

Seconds later, wildly gyrating rubber settled over her sex. Much as she needed this, it was so much. She tried to straighten then forced herself to hold still. As sensation reached every part of her, she told herself he was no longer doing anything. Except for her imprisoned arms, she had back control over her body.

Or did she?

Hot juices flowed from her, along with what was left of her ability to reason. Her head fell back so it rested on the chair. Her toes dug into the carpet, and her mouth hung open.

Back in the dungeon her mind had created over the years, staring in helpless awe and submission at the man who'd laid claim to every inch of her body. Handing herself over to him, accepting his domination, trusting.

She came. Came in a thunder of cries and clenching sex muscles. Dove into wave upon wave of defenseless heat, nearly drowned.

"I hate you!" she blurted, but it was a lie. If she hated anyone, it was herself. He now knew so much about her, nearly everything.

Chapter Ten

I wanted to point out something about the pictures you sent," Damek said. "I'm not sure you're aware of what you did. Maybe you want to talk about it."

Reno had to look at the clock to get a handle on the time. He'd barely noticed the sun setting and was surprised to learn it was going on for nine p.m. On the TV, a professional baseball game was tied, action suspended while a new pitcher warmed up.

"What?" he asked. "You're critiquing the lighting?"

"Where is she? If you're in the middle of something—"

"I'm not. What's this about?"

Damek grunted. "I just wanted to make an observation and hopefully get your reaction. Don't tell me to go to hell. Give me a minute. I might be getting to something. Have you looked at the shots you took of today's lesson?"

"No."

"You might want to."

"Damn it, what are you talking about?"

"You and I have probably taken a million pictures of slaves we're working with. After a while they all run together. Tall, short, skinny, padded, it doesn't much matter. They're naked. End of discussion."

Eventually Damek would get around to the reason for his call. In the meantime, Reno had to concentrate on bringing himself back to the here and now. He might have dozed off. That was a good enough explanation for why he was having such a hard time holding up his end of the conversation. What he did know was that his newest acquisition was lying on the couch at the opposite side of the room. A chain connected her ankle to the couch leg and her hands were cuffed in front. He'd thrown a blanket over her and her hair billowed over a throw pillow. Soft snoring sounds led him to believe she hadn't heard his cell phone.

"Something's different about this batch," Damek said. "Yeah, there were pussy and boob shots, but I don't think you've ever taken this many of a slave-in-training's face."

Reno straightened and muted the TV. "You can identify her?"

"No. Never saw her mug on a wanted poster."

Wanted poster? Had it ever gotten to that point with her? Something she'd said made him realize it was a possibility. Maybe she'd been locked up before anyone had to search for her.

"I just want to put this out there," Damek went on. "You can tell me I'm crazy if that's what you think, but I got the sense you're seeing her in a new way."

"Of course I am," he snapped. "For the first time in forever, I'm not under contract to produce a marketable product within a tight timeframe."

Damek snorted. "Maybe. Maybe not. I've been worried about you, and not just because you got smashed up good. Ever since the accident, you haven't given a damn about much of anything."

Yeah, I know.

"Are you still there? I thought you might bite my head off."

"I'm trying to decide whether it's worth the effort," he said, even though he wasn't.

"Take a look at the shots. Her expression shows in most of them."

Knowing Damek, that was as far as he'd go, which suited Reno just fine. They spent a few minutes talking baseball, then Damek said he was going to fix himself a nightcap. Reno hung up, but, instead of doing the same thing, he turned his attention to the small form on his couch. Even before she'd told him she'd spent part of her youth locked up, he'd wanted to know something about her.

He wouldn't be feeling this way if he hadn't brought her to his sanctuary.

The hell he wouldn't.

Then it had to be her innate submissive nature and the opportunity to exploit it.

No, not that either.

Angry and confused, he tried to turn his attention back to the game. The relief pitcher worked his way into a full count and kept shaking his head at the catcher's signs. After fouling off three balls, the batter walked.

"Shit," he muttered and stood. He didn't ask himself why he was going over to her. From the looks of things, she was down and out. He could wake her, of course. Hell, maybe he should, just to bring home the little issue of who was in charge, but he'd put his leg through the wringer. He should kick back in the recliner, maybe fall asleep himself.

The blanket had slid off her shoulder but still covered her breasts, which made things marginally easier on his nervous system. Frowning, he cradled his cock. It wasn't rock-hard like it had been as he'd been working on her, but neither was it just hanging there like it had ever since his accident. The docs had assured him that a loss of libido — that's what they'd called it — was normal, considering how much healing his system had to do. After all, he'd nearly died. He'd known he'd turned the corner the day he'd stopped obsessing over his mortality and started being interested in sex again.

He'd debated letting the doctors know how he earned a living. If they knew, they'd understand that being turned on was a constant condition for a man in his profession. Not giving a damn about fucking scared the hell out of him.

Maybe he should get in touch with the medical staff and let them know that the corner had been turned.

Except, maybe, the return of his hard-on was more complicated than that. Revolved around her.

His captive sighed and repositioned her hand under her

cheek. She looked so damn innocent, trusting even.

Except for the collar, cuffs, and chained ankle.

What did you do to get you sideways with the law? Did anyone stand beside you or were you alone then?

Like me.

His fingers tightened around the family jewels. Brought up short by the resultant pain, he backed away from the nameless female he'd brought into his world. Enough was enough. From now on, he'd be all business with her. Get back in the saddle, so to speak.

And once he had her the way he wanted her?

He'd worry about that then.

* * * *

"Hands behind your head. Arch your back. Stick out your breasts. Get those damn legs spread."

Despite the hobbles, Kaci struggled to obey. Otherwise, he wouldn't let her eat. He'd been doing what he called 'putting her through her paces' for what seemed like hours and showed no sign of growing tired of ordering her around. When she'd first woken after spending the night on the couch, it had taken her several minutes to absorb the reality of her situation. She hadn't had any choice but to stay in place until he'd unfastened the chain from the couch leg. He'd pushed her ahead of him into the bathroom, dragging the chain behind her. Using the toilet under his steady and silent stare had served an unnecessary reminder of their relationship.

To her relief, he'd let her use a toothbrush and wash up. She'd hoped he'd give her something for breakfast after she'd left the bathroom but he'd hobbled her.

How long ago had that been, and what else would he make her do before her training, if that's what this was, was over?

"From today forward," he said as she thrust her breasts at him, "you will have only one purpose in life. That's to please your Master. I understand your resistance. In fact, I expect it." He leaned forward and pressed the tip of the switch he'd chosen for this morning's lesson against her left nipple. "Whether you fight me or try to take your mind from what's being done to your body makes no difference. In the end, I'll win. I always do. No." He ran the switch under her chin, forcing her to lift her head. "How many times do I need to remind you to keep your position?"

She didn't think he expected a reply so concentrated on forcing her stiff muscles to do as he'd commanded. Not long ago, he'd fixed himself eggs and toast while her forehead was on the kitchen floor and her buttocks waved at nothing. The smell lingered, making her stomach growl and her mouth water, and yet, she couldn't say she hated him. She wasn't sure what she was experiencing now that they were in the living room, maybe a bit of pleasure because his day revolved around her. Everything he said and did was with her in mind.

"Hands on your thighs."

Swallowing a groan of relief, she eased her cuffed hands over her head and rested them on her upper legs. She took care to keep her back arched so, hopefully, he wouldn't give her another example of what the switch was capable of. A half-dozen stinging blows to her breasts earlier, when she hadn't presented herself to his satisfaction, had been more than enough. She guessed today's weapon was nearly four feet long and made of bamboo. Unlike what he'd used on her yesterday, it would cut flesh if he put his full strength behind it.

"Keep your hands where they are. Resist any and all impulses to touch your sex."

How did he know she was aroused?

As soon as she asked herself the question, she had the answer. This man knew everything about her — at least all the things that were important to him.

"I didn't complete yesterday's lesson," he told her. He rolled the switch between his palms. "In the greater scheme of things, this particular timing doesn't matter, but, now that I have your full attention, it's time to introduce a fundamental rule. I could get you to tell me your name, but slave suffices."

What could she do, scream at him that he was wrong? He'd only laugh and punish her.

"I dare say you have a name for me, one that starts with a B. I'm right, aren't I?"

Silence or a yes? She couldn't lie because he'd see through it.

"Hell of a dilemma, isn't it?"

Before she could think how to respond, the switch struck her upper arms. Trying to protect herself, she gasped and lifted her hands. A thin line of pain sizzled along her right thigh.

"Back in position, slave! I'm going to keep this so simple even you can follow directions. From this moment on, you will call me Master."

Master.

"Say it, now."

He'd leaned back in the chair, looking calm and relaxed, but she knew better. She still hurt where he'd struck her. Besides, what could she do, run?

No. Insane as it was, she *wanted* to be with him. Doing this.

"I'm waiting, but you know I'm not a patient man. Say it."

"Master." She stared at the floor.

"Not enough. Tell me who I am to you?"

"M-aster."

"Not enough, damn it!"

Her breasts caught fire. He stuck out his foot and pushed her off balance so she landed on her side. Curling into a ball, she risked looking up at the dominating man looming over her.

"Master," she whispered. "You're my Master."

"Exactly." He leaned down and forced her back onto her knees. "On your hands and knees like the dog you are."

Fighting anger and something else, she did as he'd commanded. She shivered when he moved behind her but didn't dare glance back at him.

"If curs have been abused, they crawl on their bellies. I can make you do that but I'd rather not."

He laid the switch lengthwise along her spine with the base on the back of her head. Obviously, he wanted her to remain with her head down for as long as it was there.

She wasn't a cur. Not yet, anyway.

"That's better." He patted her buttocks. "Now, who am I to you?"

"My Master."

"Hmm." He patted her ass again. "At least, I am unless you can get your hands on a knife or gun—either that or run. Guess what? None of those things are going to happen. I'm going to train you. Make you into what I want."

Why is that important to you?

"I'll train you to respond to your sexual nature. Eventually, that will become the only important thing."

Promise?

He was walking away. She heard the whisper of his slippers on the carpet, followed by the faint slap of rubber soles on vinyl. He'd gone into the kitchen leaving her to—to wait for her Master's return.

She would.

* * * *

"That, in a nutshell, is today's lesson. If you're going to eat, you must first please me. Call it positive reinforcement."

Master—the less she thought about what she was saying, the easier the word came—was waiting for her to perform her trick, she first had to swallow what little pride she still had. Maybe worst of all, she had no idea how long the exercise would last.

"I don't want to have to repeat myself, slave. Do it."

On the tail of a silent groan, she sat upright, placed her

143

hands on her thighs, and opened her mouth. Her knees ached even more now that she was on vinyl for the second time this morning. "Please, Master, may I have something to eat?"

"What have you done to deserve it?"

The first time he'd asked her that, she'd been at a loss for an answer. Now she knew what he wanted to hear. "I presented my ass to you for your entertainment, Master."

"That's right." He slid the switch over her buttocks. "And did doing so please me?"

"I hope so, Master."

"But you can't be sure. Why is that?"

He'd given her a total of two bites of banana, which was just enough to remind her of how starved she was.

"I don't know what you're thinking."

His faint smile died. "Oh, I believe you do."

In the short amount of time she'd been under his control, she'd learned to put all her attention into trying to read his moods. Right now, he was both impatient and disappointed. Desperate to win his approval, she mentally replayed what she'd just said.

"I don't know what you're thinking, Master."

"Better." He nodded. "You're making progress."

He was sitting on a breakfast stool, which meant she had to look up at him. Anticipating his next move made her sweat.

"You asked me something a minute ago," he said. "What was it?"

"Please, Master, I would be grateful if you fed me."

"Fed you? Are you saying you can't do it yourself?"

Stifling the urge to snap 'no' rendered her incapable of speech. Then something in his eyes, a glint maybe, reminded her that he was committed to teaching her.

Please show me how to please you.

"You told me not to use my hands, Master." She indicated the metal around her wrists and the short chain connecting them.

"Yes, I did." He rubbed the switch against the side of her neck above the collar that now felt as if it were part of her. "But that was only one half of the terms under which I'd provide you with nourishment. What is the rest?"

She had to close her eyes to keep her confusion from showing. She wanted to get onto her hands and knees and present him with her ass, but he'd ordered her to keep her fingers on her thighs. Her mouth carefully neutral, she awkwardly scooted around so her back was to him. Then, fingers digging into her thighs, she lowered her forehead to the floor.

Would demeaning herself never end?

Did she want to?

"Good action on your part, pet." He groaned, and she guessed he'd stood up. Hopefully, once she'd earned the right to know, he'd tell her what had happened to him and what it had done to him. Let her ease the memories. "There will be times I'll expect you to make decisions not just respond to commands. I'm glad to see you're still capable of doing so."

What was he getting ready to do? Whatever it was, it must have something to do with her so-accessible bung hole. Maybe she didn't want to eat after all. Anything to put an end to this terrible test of wills she was in no position to win.

More than a test. Fundamental change.

"Some of the Dominants who employ Carnal's services are fans of the pony lifestyle," he said from behind and above her. "They want their slaves trained to race and participate in other competitions. Needless to say, part of our training involves teaching slaves to conduct themselves like horses. That includes wearing bits and bridles."

She wasn't hearing this! No way could he be thinking of turning her into—she couldn't finish the thought.

"I've trained my share of ponies." He placed his splayed fingers over her buttocks and kneaded them. Confusing her even more. "At the beginning I wasn't sure I was the right trainer for the job, but I enjoy learning new skills. It gives me...purpose." He paused. "One of my favorite tasks involved giving a pony a tail."

Even before he pressed a finger against her puckered opening, she knew what he was going to do. She whined but didn't move.

"I haven't decided whether I'll take you down that road. If I do, this is what you have to get used to."

She needed to relax but couldn't. Any second, he'd shove his finger into that dark and private place. Become part of her.

Seemingly oblivious to her turmoil, he lightly rubbed her there. This wasn't her! Surely she hadn't gone from paying her bills to kneeling naked and submissive before a man she now called Master, a man intent on demonstrating ownership of her.

But she was and he was.

All she could do was feel.

React.

Right now, he was being gentle. That might change at any moment, but holding on to sanity meant burying herself in the here and now. Turning her body over to him.

"You have the makings of a true submissive." His voice was seductive. "You're fighting that side of your nature, but I know how to change things. In fact, I know you better than you do yourself."

Was that a tease or a warning? Whichever it was, she didn't dare move since he held the upper hand in all ways. Besides, oh, God, besides that the light brush of finger over her ass opening felt good, an escape from reality.

Master had been gone for days, but not before tethering her to the stair railing. The neck chain was long enough that she'd been able to move from room to room. She'd filled the lonely hours reading, watching TV, and studying what she'd been able to see outside the picture window. The door had been locked from the outside, of course and he'd taken care not to leave her with any way of getting in touch with the rest of the world.

Her world? That's what he'd become before he'd left her alone. She had no existence beyond him, cared nothing for her life beyond what he'd created.

And now he was back. Ready for his slave to service him. Willing to let her curl herself around him and kiss him in gratitude for things she barely understood.

"You're zoning," Master said as his finger drank from the juices coating her labia. "Going deep inside yourself and finding what you need."

She didn't care what he said, just that he was talking to her, touching her now, coating her bung hole, entering — entering, slowly going deeper.

"Master, please."

"Please what, slave? I'm not going to hurt you, at least not now. You need food, but you haven't yet done enough to earn it. Stay with me. Acknowledge what's happening. Make my mastery of you your world."

Did she want to do that? The longer his finger remained in her ass, the better it felt. A lifetime ago, she'd created scenarios in her mind about being a sex slave. She'd tailored the scenarios of take and give to meet her private need. This was different. So different. She had no control over what Master might do, how he viewed her body, what he needed and would take from it.

But she'd embrace these moments when her ass was offered to him, her forehead rested on the hard floor, metal constrained her limbs, and his collar circled her neck.

"You're my pony," he whispered. "I've entered you in a race and expect you to make me proud. I've placed a wager that you'll come in first and am decorating you so everyone will know what you are to me. You'll wear my tail, proudly."

Pressure built as the invasion deepened. In her mind's eye, his finger became a high, proud golden tail. Once he secured it inside her to his satisfaction, he'd parade her before the other pony Masters. Scared and excited, she'd prance, her knees high, head back, bridle ringing her face, and bit protruding from both sides of her mouth. Others would note the red leather finery crisscrossing her naked body. The instant Master snapped his whip, she'd break into a gallop.

"Are you a runner, slave? What good, other than satisfying me, are you?"

She hadn't expected the question. Before now, she'd concentrated on trying to understand him and herself. Exploring the depths of their relationship was beyond her.

"Have I satisfied you, Master? You haven't…"

"Fucked you. That's what you were going to say, weren't you?"

"It's going to happen."

"Yes, it is."

She waited for him to continue, but he went on manipulating her ass. He repeatedly transferred lubricant from her pussy to her other hole, making sure her juices coated both her rear entrance and deep inside. Part of her stood behind Master watching him work, but mostly she remained acutely aware of every inch of her submissive body. He was in charge. She'd let him do whatever he wanted to her. She had no choice—and these moments fascinated her.

Excited her.

"Maybe you would make a decent pony. It's something I should consider, starting with this."

His finger had been buried as far as it would go, both alarming and intriguing her. He slowly pulled out. She sensed he was about to change things. Something new pressed against her puckered flesh. It started to spin, sliding past taut muscles and probing, probing. Whatever it was, it was harder, wider, more insistent than his finger.

"What— Please, Master what—?"

"Be quiet and experience."

The pressure was relentless, which made doing what he'd ordered nearly impossible. Despite the apprehension threatening to take over, she knew he intended to force whatever it was inside her. This was his idea of a horse tail. She shivered at the thought of how the thing must look sticking out from her, quivering every time her ass muscles clenched.

She concentrated on what was inside her until she realized he'd plugged her with what he'd used earlier to whip her.

Burying the switch to his satisfaction seemed to take forever, but finally the probing ended. So much blood had rushed to her temples that her head throbbed. Her back ached. He slapped her buttocks.

"Lift your head. Present yourself like a well-trained horse."

I hate…

No, she didn't.

Getting her arms to accept the weight of her upper body took concentration, and yet she remained acutely aware of how stuffed she was back there. How changed. She started to look behind her.

"Don't! Your appearance is no concern of yours. The only thing that's important is whether your Master is pleased. Crawl to the living room."

When he'd ordered her back into the kitchen, she'd hoped it was with the intention of feeding her. Maybe he no longer cared whether she had anything to eat, except part of a banana, but, given what he'd just done to her, it didn't matter to her, either.

Crawling with her arms and legs restrained was hard enough, but that was nothing compared to the feel of something rammed in her bung hole. The switch was so long that it bounced and waved with her every move. It didn't hurt, and the almost constant vibrations spread to her pussy. Enveloped it. Did Master know how closely this sensation resembled what the overpowered vibrator had felt like? At least, thankfully, she told herself as she plodded into the living room, the whip couldn't tease a climax from her.

Could it?

Master was behind her, undoubtedly amusing himself by watching his newly minted slave pony.

Shame pressed around her, became a weight.

A gift.

"Don't you have any pride in yourself? There's nothing graceful about the way you move. Your body is your most valuable possession. Treat it with respect."

He expected her to prance around? She was dirty and hungry. Her hair hung in damp strands around her sweat-stained face. Bad as the restraints were, the thing protruding from her ass would make the people from his world laugh.

"Maybe you don't have what it takes to be a show pony. Maybe I'll put a yoke on you and turn you into a plow animal. Give you long ears and call you my mule."

If she was such a failure, why was he spending his time with her? He should cast her out, let her go.

No, he wouldn't. He'd sell her to someone who wanted a mule, a broken whore.

Something beyond fear overruled humiliation, and she lifted her head. The man who'd captured her was harsh and relentless, but so far, he hadn't been cruel. Another Master might not have his — his what, humanity?

"What's it going to be, slave? Do you want to be taught what it takes to please me? Maybe you'd rather take your chances with someone else?"

They were once again in the room that spoke of male and masculinity. She was his tethered sex slave. He loomed over her, in charge.

Trembling, she turned and looked up at him. He needed a shave. "What must I learn, Master?"

Chapter Eleven

'What must I learn, Master?' To the best of his recollection, none of his previous trainees had asked him that, especially so early in their lessons. Granted, Carnal rules stipulated that new captives not be allowed to speak until their transformation had begun, but he still believed this one was unique. He also didn't think that plugging her rear hole and calling her a pony had been wholly responsible.

Within a few minutes of her question, he'd gone back into the kitchen for some cereal and had fed her one piece at a time. Keeping her on her hands and knees with the switch in her had undoubtedly reminded her of her place in his world. Reminded him, as well. After toying with it for a while, he'd drawn the switch out of her and she'd immediately thanked him. She'd obviously hated kissing the moist base he'd pressed against her lips, but she'd done it.

Now, as she stood beside him while he adjusted the water temperature in the downstairs shower, he tried to assess where she was on her journey to submission. It wasn't going to be a smooth transformation, but neither did he anticipate the kind of resistance he'd gotten from some of the subjects who'd come before her.

Subject, or something more? Beyond a simple slave?

"Wait," he warned as she started to step into the shower. "We're doing this my way. Hold out your hands."

She hesitated, which was long enough for him to get the unspoken message. She didn't trust him.

Would she ever? "Your body belongs to me." He reached into his pocket, withdrew a key, and unfastened the cuff around her left hand. Then he spun her away from him and drew her arms behind her. She tensed but didn't resist while he re-cuffed her hands. The hobbles were still around her ankles, and he had no intention of taking off the collar.

He pushed her into the shower and positioned her under the spray. As water streamed over her hair, she tried to look out from behind the wet curtain at him. He pulled off his shirt then hesitated. Once he got rid of his jeans, she'd see the still-healing scars, which he'd intended to put off for a few more days.

To hell with it!

Naked, he stepped into the small shower and swiped her hair back from her face. Water sluiced over her breasts, flowed over her belly, disappeared between her legs. His cock responded.

He wetted the washcloth he'd brought in with him and rubbed soap over it. Maybe that, in part, was why he'd taken her, because he'd known it would take pressing against a naked female to remind his cock of what it was capable of.

As for other reasons—they had too much to do with solitude.

She stared at the thick spear jutting at her.

"That represents a great deal of what our relationship's about." But not all.

Was that a nod? He couldn't be sure.

Done with trying to decipher her thoughts, he concentrated on washing every inch of her well-toned body. After that furtive glance at his erection, she stared at the shower wall. Did she really think she could divorce herself from what he was doing to her simply by not looking at him?

He was her worst nightmare and, depending on a lot of things, he might become her most treasured reality.

With that possibility in mind, he pushed her still-soapy body into a corner and slipped the washcloth over her inner legs. She clamped them together.

"No," he warned. "Shit, you know better."

Thinking to keep her off balance, he adjusted the spray so it was concentrated on the top of her head. Her hair covered her face, blinding her. He left her to try to get enough air in her lungs and turned his attention to something he could practically do in his sleep.

He'd often demanded that slaves describe what being sexually aroused felt like, but, even after they'd spilled everything, he'd known he'd never be able to truly get inside their minds and bodies. One thing he was sure of, repeatedly rubbing her pussy would get to this one. Break her down.

Help her understand the meaning of Master.

It didn't happen at first, but little by little, she relaxed. Her knees occasionally buckled, forcing her to struggle to regain her balance. She no longer tried to shield her pussy from him. In fact, she'd opened herself to him. The back of her head now rested on the shower wall, her mouth sagged, and her breathing was ragged. She pushed her pelvis at him so he planted his free hand over her belly and shoved. It wasn't that he didn't want her surrender, he wanted to make clear who was in charge.

For both of them.

She kept trying to look down at herself. With that much water plastering her hair to her face, she couldn't see much.

That was fine with him. Her attention should be fixed on something else.

He'd given her pussy a brisk rubbing since he wanted her to be as sensitive as possible. Going by her body language, he'd reached his goal. Switching tactics, he let up on the pressure so the soft terrycloth barely grazed her swollen labia. He occasionally subjected her clit to a bit of attention but was careful to keep things brief. He wanted her on edge and hungry. As for granting her satisfaction, well, he hadn't made up his mind about that.

He left her to pant and frown while he re-soaped the cloth. Instead of returning to what he'd been doing, however, he coated her breasts. Before, he hadn't treated them to anything except abuse. After an initial whimper and a straightening of her spine, she sagged. He concentrated on giving each breast equal attention. Just thinking about what it must feel like for her got him all hot and bothered again. He closed his fingers around his cock.

Good. So damn good. Like coming back to life.

The amount of time they'd spent in the shower didn't matter. Then the hot water started to run out. Thinking to turn the handle all the way to H, he let go of himself. That was all it took to remember that right now was about turning her into something new. Grunting, he ran his hand over her legs, swept aside her sex lips, and slid his middle finger into her. Continuing to stimulate her breasts at the same time took concentration, but he was used to this particular maneuver. Most of the time, he'd first gotten a slave into the mood via a liberal dose of pain, but there wasn't anything wrong with improvising.

With treating her differently.

"Feels good, doesn't it? Good and a little scary. Your Master can do anything he wants, which means you don't dare trust him, but you don't want him to stop. Confused, you tell yourself you'll live in the moment, take what pleasure you can."

"It-it's getting cold."

She was right. Fortunately for him, the spray was directed at her. Figuring goosebumps were her problem, he dropped the washcloth and fastened thumb and forefinger around her right nipple. He pulled down.

"Master?"

"Master what? You think I'm going to tell you what I have in mind? Ain't gonna happen."

He let up the pressure, even lightly massaged the trapped nub while pumping her hole.

"Not fair. Damn it, not fair."

Of course it wasn't. That had never been his intention. He stopped his assault on her sex long enough to turn off the water then rammed his victim — victim, now there was an interesting word — into the corner. He stopped all pretense at arousal and went straight for assault. By turn he grabbed one breast then the other, flattening them against her chest wall while kneading the full, rich mounds. The hand between her legs threatened to cramp. He backed off but continued his attack on her pussy.

Let her experience forced sexual awakening.

Make her his.

"You can't, you can't," she chanted. Her legs gave up the fight and she would have fallen if not for him. He was getting cold — and hungry for something he'd nearly forgotten he needed.

Make her pay for everything that had gone wrong in his world. Make her experience the depth of helplessness as he had. Finger-fuck her into unconsciousness if necessary. Take her somewhere she'd never been.

"Master, oh, Master!"

She shuddered. The nearly graceful spasms increased. Her head thrashed and the muscles in her shoulders and arms knotted as she strained to free her hands. Staying with her, keeping her in Hell and Heaven, he watched as she climaxed. As she started to come down, he redoubled his attack and sent her to a higher level. She sounded as if she were dying. Her muscles jumped and trembled.

He understood women's bodies so well he knew the exact moment she'd reached her limit. Her sex might've continued to clench, but she was no longer aware of anything. She wasn't unconscious as much as emotionally overloaded. Responsibility for the helpless creature kicked in, prompting him to hoist her onto his shoulder and step out of the shower. His damaged leg protested. Surrendering to the pain, he put her down and pointed at the stairs. "Up, now," he commanded.

She gave him a drunken look. Cursing, he returned to the bathroom for the cuffs key and freed her legs.

"Up," he repeated.

Saying nothing, she obeyed.

He followed, not once taking his gaze off his slave's body. "Onto the bed," he commanded.

Shaking with cold and things she probably couldn't define, she complied and stared up at him. He left her long enough to return to go into his private bathroom for a couple of towels. After throwing one over her, he dried himself. She curled onto her side and tried to burrow into the spread.

"You..." She swallowed. "You made me..."

"Climax? Yeah, I did. It won't be the last time."

A look of dread and anticipation passed over her. Her attention settled on his erection. Now that he was dry, he debated doing the same to her but didn't. Still naked, he spun her around so her back was to him and unfastened one wrist cuff.

"You're my servant, not the other way around," he informed her. "Get dry."

The cuffs still dangled from her right wrist and got in the way as she sat up and did as he'd commanded, beginning with her face. After reaching her waist, she slid off the bed and rubbed her hips, buttocks, and legs. She didn't touch her crotch, undoubtedly because she was too sensitive there. Finally, she wrapped the towel around her hair. Her hands fluttered over her naked body.

"Master?"

"What?"

She stared at the floor. "May I speak?"

"It depends on what you say."

"I...thank you."

He hadn't expected that. Slaves-in-training went to great lengths trying to hide how deeply climaxing impacted them. Instead of acknowledging how good coming felt, they blamed him and the other trainers.

"For what? Giving you a shower?"

Her mouth was working, giving rise to the suspicion that she was debating whether to agree with him. He wasn't sure he wanted the communication to continue but he'd lived with silence for so long.

"Not just that." Her attention left the floor and slowly moved up his legs. That was something else he seldom saw in a slave. Most times, they did everything they could not to acknowledge a trainer's existence.

Her gaze locked on his scarred leg. He half believed she could see through the layers to the metal rods that would be part of him for as long as he lived. How would she react if she knew he'd nearly bled to death?

"Don't," he warned. "That's none of your concern."

"But—"

"I'm not going to say it again. My scars are my business, not yours. What, slave, were you going to thank me for?"

Tearing her attention off the still-red proof of several surgeries, Kaci concentrated on Master's cock. She'd already grown accustomed to being naked while he remained fully clothed, so seeing him in the same condition was something new she had to get used to. His nudity might not have made as much as an impact if she hadn't recently survived the most out-of-control climax of her life. Just thinking of how his hands had commanded her helpless body kicked up her heart rate. If she relived the relentless race to the cliff he'd forced her over, she might find herself there again.

The damp leather collar he'd locked her into remained in place and it would be too easy for him to refasten the cuffs. Proof of his mastery touched, not just her flesh, but had seeped deeply into her.

Was changing her.

"You made me come," she whispered, still focused on his dark erection. "You...you knew how to make... I had no control..."

"Get used to it."

'Get used to it.' But why would he concentrate on her sexual surrender? His sexual needs hadn't been met.

"I don't know if I can. I never...I've had fantasies, but they never..." Damn it, what was so hard about expressing

157

gratitude?

This was real. Today wasn't some crazy example of her imagination gone wild. Thanks to him, her existence had changed at the most fundamental level.

"What kind of fantasies?" he demanded.

"Nothing." Why had she said anything? "I didn't mean—"

"Yes, you did. Tell me about them."

"It was crazy stuff. Just...I don't know."

"The hell you don't. You sometimes turned to them to satisfy your sexual needs, the kind of needs I dealt with as I made you climax."

'Climax.' Pleasure in the midst of—no, it hadn't been a nightmare.

She might regret using action to express what she didn't have the words for. Despite the warning voice clawing at her senses, she unwrapped the towel and finger-combed her hair. Standing before him without shrinking away might be the hardest thing she'd ever done. At the same time, his body continued to sing its siren song. This man who insisted she call him Master hadn't simply forced her to climax. He'd introduced her to something wonderful. Exciting. Freeing even.

Was that it? For a few incredible seconds, she'd separated herself from whoever she was and had become a new woman. A sexual creature capable of unbelievable pleasure.

Confusion, physical attraction, and the humming throughout her spun together. Giving in to all three, she sank to her knees on the thick carpet and crawled toward him. He'd devoted time and attention to teaching her how to present herself to a Master and she used what she'd learned to control her body's movements. She held her head low and her back so straight his switch wouldn't have fallen off. At the same time, she made her breasts sway and kept her legs apart.

She couldn't say how long it took her to reach him. All she knew was the journey had both taken forever and ended too soon. He smelled of clean male. A few droplets of moisture clung to his pubic hair. She licked. Out of the corner of her eye she saw his fingers knot. The collar clung to her neck, while the single cuff served as a reminder of how easy it would be for him to do anything he wanted to her.

He already had, she reminded herself and, again, licked. She didn't care about his reasons for sending her hurtling in release. Only acknowledging how much things had changed about her world registered.

Her gratitude.

Master.

She turned her head and brushed her cheek against the side of his cock. He took hold of her hair but didn't pull her away. The only sound came from their harsh breaths. Saliva flooded her mouth, forcing her to swallow repeatedly before she trusted herself to touch her lips to his cock head. The sweet salty taste of pre-cum filled her. Craving another taste, she opened her mouth and took a half inch of him into her.

"You're my slave," he muttered. "Don't for a moment forget that."

"I won't. I can't."

In another time and in a different world, she'd had sex with other men. She'd even performed fellatio. Afterward, she'd asked the men if the act had lived up to their expectations. Their responses had danced around the issue and the relationships hadn't lasted long enough for her to decide whether she wanted to work on her technique.

It was different now. More was at stake.

Closing her eyes, she mentally turned herself over to this man who'd said he owned her. His accident had been traumatic, different from what being behind bars had been like for her, and yet the same in some respects. This man would never admit to being afraid, especially not to her, but surely there'd been moments — maybe more than just moments — when he hadn't known whether he'd live.

He had. He deserved to celebrate life.

With the help of the woman at his feet.

Overwhelmed by the promise she wasn't sure she could or wanted to keep, she nevertheless moistened her lips and slid them over his length. Maybe having her eyes closed was what was making her dizzy, but it was safer this way. She could touch and taste him, not have to try to make sense of his expression.

Or herself.

His fingers remained locked around her hair and acted as a conduit to his tension, his anticipation. At any moment, he might immobilize her head and ram his cock down her throat, but this was now. Them. Her gratitude.

Her dreams of sexual slavery had revolved around her Master controlling her every movement and pain, lots of pain. Maybe that's why she was having such a hard time acknowledging this small mastery over him.

That was it! Instead of making this act about her thankfulness, she'd fall back on familiar scenarios. Find a moment of safety.

In her mind, he clipped a chain to her collar and pulled her so close to his groin that her nose smashed against his flat belly. He held a whip in his free hand and occasionally lashed her exposed buttocks. Either she pleased him or he'd punish her.

Maybe he would, anyway.

Excited, she opened her mouth wide. Now, he tasted not just of soap, but also of power. Her body was his to punish and force, her mouth had only one purpose.

Eyes still resolutely closed, she tightened her lips around his length and lifted and lowered her head. Master needed stimulation, so she'd give it to him, suckle, nibble, and lick. All the while, she'd remain in tune with his reactions, judging and anticipating, giving, always giving.

Filled with purpose, she leaned into him, took him deeper. However, despite her best efforts at self-mastery, she gagged the instant his tip touched the back of her throat.

"You're worthless! If you don't do any better than that, I'll make you regret you were born."

Anchored by Master's imagined warning, she swallowed and concentrated on giving his cock complete access. She kept her mouth loose, her mind both open and empty. Survival depended on worshiping Master's cock, putting its pleasure before breathing, even.

Her throat relaxed. There was nothing beyond his heat, weight, and length. His cock's swollen veins and silky head became her everything.

Delight and surrender grew as she leaned even closer. Deeper and deeper, his hard organ pushing into her throat, closing off her ability to breathe, making her part of him. His hair-hold tightened. A sense of fulfillment flooded her. He wanted this. So did she. She'd pass out for him, die if that's what brought him pleasure.

Her temples pulsed. Her head threatened to burst. With the sensations came a primitive instinct for survival, prompting her to shake her head in an attempt to break free. He slackened his hold, and she relaxed her mouth muscles. He slid out. Then she pulled in air that smelled of him. The instant her mind cleared, her desire to put him first reasserted itself. She opened her eyes and acknowledged the man who'd become her world.

"I'm sorry," she whispered. "Please, let me try again."

"Why does it matter?"

"You gave me pleasure. I want to do the same for you."

His puzzled expression prompted her to replay what she'd just told him. Of course, he didn't believe her? Not trying to explain herself, something she wasn't sure she could do, she moistened her tongue and lathed his length. As he stroked her hair, she wondered if he really thought of her as his pet.

She no longer cared. Even if she didn't understand the transformation, she was who she was. Rather than taking him back into her, she nibbled and licked. He still controlled her, but she wanted it like that. Needed it.

A small voice demanded to know if she'd lost her mind. Determined to silence it, she renewed her efforts to please him. She settled her hand over his base and anchored his cock. Touching what was precious to him emboldened her. Keeping her actions slow and measured, she again turned her head and nipped at his length. After several moments of pretending she was about to eat him, she kissed where her teeth had been. He still held on to her hair.

This was right, good, Master and slave, pleasure given and taken. The longer she tended to him, the more her own sexual need asserted itself. When she couldn't hold off any more, she slipped her free hand between her legs and stroked herself. Had she ever been this wet?

"Do it. Mouth fuck me."

Without taking her fingers from her sex hole, she stretched her mouth wide and guided his hard length back into the heated cave that was her gift to him. She closed her lips around him, sucked.

Groans ripped through him as he released her hair and clamped his fingers around her shoulders. As he began thrusting, she let go of his cock and gripped her breast.

Master was so strong! Even though she tried to grab some of his strength for herself, she weakened. Lost her separate self.

She became Master's tool, her mouth an orifice with only one purpose, to bring him pleasure. To take whatever he hurled at her. He repeatedly rammed into her, his thrusts coming so fast and hard she couldn't draw breath.

Please him. Live for him. Be what he needs.

Master wasn't some teenage boy pumped full of testosterone, so she expected his release to take a few minutes. She was still trying to accustom herself to his fast and powerful rhythm when sweet cum flooded her mouth. He cursed. If anything, his attack intensified.

Take me with you. Let me feel what you are.

Something winked out in her. She no longer saw herself as separate from Master. With his discharge sliding down her throat came the belief that they'd become one. She shuddered, gasped. Tears burned. Her pussy muscles

spasmed.
  Coming. Feeding off him.
  Winning.
  Losing.

Chapter Twelve

"You're moving fast," Damek said.

"It isn't just me." Reno kicked back his recliner and looked at the nearby window. It was light out, but whether it was morning or afternoon he wasn't sure. He had vague memories of ordering the slave to stay on her knees, locking her wrist to the bed leg, handing her a throw, and crawling under the covers for the rest he hadn't gotten last night, because he'd spent it watching her sleep. He had no idea how long he'd napped before getting dressed and coming downstairs for something to eat. "This trainee's on a fast track."

"Have you decided what you're going to do with her?"

"No," he enunciated carefully. "I haven't. What's it to you?"

"Maybe you're where I was not long ago."

Damek was talking about the woman who'd started out simply being a job, but now lived with him. The two traveled together, and just last month they'd climbed Mt. Shasta in northern California. She wore his collar, but their relationship was unlike any Reno had ever seen between Master and slave. They genuinely cared for each other while maintaining their roles. Damek had cut back on his Carnal work and had been talking about starting his own business working with natural submissives who wanted to live up to their Masters' expectations.

Not long after Reno had begun physical therapy, Damek had asked him to at least consider joining him. At the time he'd been so wrapped up in getting through one day—and night—at a time that he'd turned Damek down without a moment's thought.

Maybe he should do some thinking.

About a lot of things.

"What do you know about her?" Damek asked.

"Not much." She was still upstairs because he needed a little time apart from her. "From what she said, I'm thinking she was a juvenile delinquent. Apparently, she spent a long time locked up."

"I'd think the last thing she'd want is to be restrained again." Damek had made a good point.

"I don't have a cage here and I haven't tried putting her in a closet, so I can't say—"

"What about basic bondage or whippings? Does she freak out?"

"No."

Damek grunted. "She would, unless she wants this."

"You're saying you believe she's a submissive?"

"You know her better than I do."

I'm trying.

"Look, I'm not going to give you suggestions. You know what you're doing as well as I do, but if it was me I'd be pushing her limits. Taking her past those limits to see how she reacts."

"Breaking her?"

"Is that what you want?"

Damn Damek for trying to play shrink. "What did you call for? I have better things to do than flap my gums talking to you."

"Sure you do." A sigh reached him across the miles. "I'm just checking up. You want the truth? Ever since your accident it's been like trying to talk to a dead man. Sounds as if you're starting to get over it."

Maybe I am. "How are things going at Carnal? Have they set a date for that international auction?"

"It's going to take place in a couple of weeks. Thomas asked if you'd said anything about showing up for it."

Thomas—everyone knew that wasn't Carnal

Incorporated's vice president's real name—had shown up at the hospital a few days after the accident, but Reno didn't remember much about the visit. Since then, their communication had been limited to Thomas explaining that Carnal's insurance carrier intended to wait to see how many of his medical bills his motorcycle insurance would cover before stepping up.

"What'd you tell him?"

"To fuck off."

"No, you didn't."

"No, but I wanted to. He'll die a prick. I told him to send you an invitation. I'm trying to decide whether watching the auction will get you off the fence about going back to work."

A naked female waited for him upstairs. Not long ago, he'd ejaculated for the first time since he'd nearly lost his life. What mattered was seeing if that would happen again—and learning more about the creature who'd made it happen.

The slave who'd climaxed from making him come.

"We've already discussed this."

"Yeah, kind of. You can agree, disagree, or tell me to mind my own damn business. You sound different since you got your hands on her, more alive."

He pressed the heel of his hand against his cock. "Maybe I am."

A minute later, he closed down his cell phone and stared at the stairs. The conversation had worn him out. At the same time, he acknowledged that Damek was right. He *did* feel different—and that unnerved him.

Knowing he was well on the road to recovery was a hell of a lot better than struggling to get through days framed by physical therapy and nightmares had been. The thing he still couldn't, and didn't want, to wrap his mind around was how much nearly dying had changed him inside.

Wanting something different from life.

Enough!

He stood and headed up to where he'd left her. Every step brought back memories of his struggle to climb the damn stairs right after he'd gotten out of the hospital. He'd been glad he had the cabin to himself so no one could watch him crawl, or hear his pain-filled gasps. Some things a man needed to get through on his own.

Sometimes solitude could be a bitch.

He opened the bedroom door and looked at the naked woman on his bed. He wasn't alone today. Time to learn who and what she was.

* * * *

"Thank you, Master," Kaci whispered. Now that she'd used the toilet and washed her hands, she wasn't sure what to do. This bathroom was larger than the one downstairs, all silver, white, and black. Expensive. Masculine.

While waiting for him to free her, she'd half convinced herself he'd want sex again. The possibilities were endless — he might spread eagle her on the bed and pump her helpless body, he might order her back onto her hands and knees and take her from behind, maybe he'd command her to suck his cock again, but she hoped not because she needed him in her.

He studied her from the doorway. His relentless stare unnerved her. At the same time, having his attention locked on her heated her veins.

She didn't want to be like this. To have her existence revolve around him. To be so vulnerable.

Yes, she did.

"Where were you born?" he asked.

She blinked. "San Diego."

"Where did you grow up?"

Don't let him in. "We — My parents moved around a lot. They, ah, they weren't always together. During separations, my mother took us to be near her aunt."

"How did you feel about the way you lived?"

Old resentments reasserted themselves. At the same time, she wished she could find a way to change the subject. Knowing he was interested in her past, her emotions, scared her. Wasn't living in the moment with this man emotionally unnerving enough?

"I, um, I didn't think about it much. It was just the way things were."

"I don't believe you."

He'd seen through her attempt to avoid painful issues, but was that surprising? After all, she stood before him naked, except for his restraints. Even though she hadn't looked at the cuff again hanging from her wrist since he'd returned, she couldn't ignore its impact.

"What do you want me to say?" she asked.

"The truth. About everything."

Not fair! She wasn't ready for this, couldn't imagine ever being. And yet it had been so long since anyone had cared about her. "I didn't like having to change schools, but that happens to a lot of children, so it's hardly remarkable."

"We're not talking about other people. This is about you." He stepped into her space, gathered up the loose cuff and slipped it around her free wrist. Just like that, he'd handcuffed her again, reinforcing his mastery of her. "What about siblings?"

"Two older brothers."

"Are you in touch with them?"

Maybe he was trying to determine whether they'd look for her. She could lie, try to convince him that keeping her was dangerous, but what if he learned the truth? That might anger him and the fragile connection she believed had begun between them would be shattered.

"Hardly ever. They joined the military as soon as they could." She studied the floor. "They couldn't wait to leave home."

"Is that what you did? You packed your belongings and took off?"

"No. I..."

"What?"

As irritated as he sounded, she should tell him what he wanted to know, but he was asking so much of her.

Just do it.

"Shortly after I turned sixteen, I was found guilty of a crime and taken to a juvenile detention center."

"You were hauled out of your parents' home? Did they try to protect you?"

The question was laughable. Somehow he'd seen deep into her, seen scars she'd hoped no one ever would. The more he learned, the more vulnerable she'd become. She'd have no defenses left, nothing to keep away from this man who believed she belonged to him.

Own. Belonging.

"Answer me! Did your parents come to your defense?"

Her mouth worked but nothing came out. She felt backed into a corner.

"Answer!"

Suddenly, irrationally, she launched herself at him. Lifting her arms, she tried to jam the cuffs' chain against his throat. He grabbed her and spun her around. Then, to her surprise, he let go.

"Go on, try to get away!"

"No!" she screamed. Lowering her head so it was aimed at his middle, she charged him. She must have caught him unaware, because she hit where she'd intended. He grunted and stumbled back a step. Determined to push off him, she braced her arms on his chest. Before she could, his vise-like fingers clamped around her forearms.

Forcing her arms over her head, he backed her away from him. She kicked out and connected with his left leg. A hissing groan escaped him.

I'm sorry.

"Damn you! God damn!"

She wasn't sure how it happened, but he levered her so her back was to him. He again pushed her tethered arms over her head and, holding on to the cuffs, marched her toward the bed. The way his breathing labored, she had no doubt he was still in pain.

He shoved her. She landed face down on the bed. Desperate as she was to get away, fear of angering him even more than he was slowed her. Before she could decide what to do, as if she had any options, he hoisted her onto the mattress and rammed what she guessed was his good leg against her. Her arms remained over her head, and with his hand over the back of her neck, she couldn't straighten.

"I'll teach you to try to defy me." Every word struck her like a blow.

I'm sorry. Master, I'm sorry. Despite her dread of him, however, she couldn't make herself apologize. Not only was it too late, she needed him to understand what had compelled her to do what she had.

"You will tell me what I want to hear," he spat out the words. "That's what this lesson is about, you being honest about everything."

That's how you'll demonstrate your mastery over me.

Understanding how important keeping the upper hand was to him distracted her from what he was doing. Besides, she couldn't stop him.

After shoving down on her neck to make it clear that he expected her to stay in place, he uncuffed one hand, drew her arms behind her, and re-secured her. To her surprise, he massaged her buttocks. Expecting a tirade, she held her breath, but he only kneaded. Despite herself, she responded. Then he pulled one ass cheek away from the other and ran his nail over her rear opening.

She moaned and squirmed.

"What are you saying, slave? That maybe you don't want to run away?"

"Yes, I do!" Why hadn't she called him Master?

"Don't lie to me, or yourself."

He kicked her legs apart, planted his hand on her pussy, and stroked. She stopped trying to get out from under him. She was upset over his ability to control her responses, but she lacked the will to do anything about it. It shouldn't be like this! She'd spent years living on her own. The last thing she'd ever do again, she'd repeatedly told herself, was let a man have the upper hand. Once had been enough. Once had nearly destroyed her.

"Don't, please," she begged as a finger entered her drenched opening. "I don't want—"

"Your mind hates what's happening, but it isn't in charge, slave. Something baser is, something I know a great deal about."

She knew better than to believe he was no longer angry at her. Any moment, he might start punishing her, but right now his finger was working in and out, pumping her, making her pussy weep in anticipation. Tearing her apart.

"That's right," he all but crooned. "Give up. Let it happen. Embrace your submission."

I don't want to do this, I don't! Why, then, were her cheeks on fire? Why did she ache with the need to have his cock inside her?

Because he no longer was holding onto the back of her neck. That hand had moved to between her buttocks. His thumb pushed on her bung hole. His other hand remained at her pussy, so now—oh, damn yes—now two fingers filled her.

An image expanded to fill what was left of her mind. Master had claimed ownership of her ass and cunt. Robbed of the use of her hands, and face down on the bed that smelled and felt of him, she had no voice in what was happening.

Could only experience.

Rubbing, invading and retreating, Master's breath hot on her back and both of his legs now touching her thighs. Attacking. Taking her down.

Tearing her apart.

Fulfilling her.

Anticipation grew. Despite her attempts to remain silent, she bleated. Every time he withdrew his fingers from her sex, she wailed in fear of being denied. She hated and loved being plundered.

A lifetime ago her teenage sex drive had nearly destroyed her. She'd spent so long denying its power while carving out an existence she could handle. Today Master was teaching her how futile those attempts had been.

Sexual need ruled her.

Master ruled her.

"Please, please, please," she whimpered.

"Please stop doing this or make you climax?"

Not let but make. That should be her warning, her call to action. Why then was she allowing him to demean her?

As her body softened and heated, her mind went back through the years to the day a clanging door signified the end to freedom. At first she'd screamed and kicked the door, but once she'd exhausted herself, a measure of sanity had returned. She had no choice but to endure.

That's what she'd do now, endure.

Not lose herself in pleasure.

Somehow.

Despite the hot pressure in her pussy and commanding thumb pushing past her puckered flesh, she forcefully gathered bits and pieces from her past. Stern looks from those whose job it had been to teach her the error of her ways, writing her parents but never hearing from them, begging to be allowed to contact the man-boy she'd been in love with, only to be given a letter from him saying he was moving on, getting married.

Realizing what a fool she'd been.

"Where'd you go?" Master turned her over and pulled her off the bed. Her legs shook, her pussy still dripped, and everything was empty. "How did you manage to check out?"

He took hold of her chin and forced her to face him, but she didn't answer.

"I don't understand you, slave. However, I'm going to."

Chapter Thirteen

A few minutes later, Kaci stood on the second-story deck outside Master's bedroom. Seeing the trees standing guard around his place brought home their isolation. She'd barely had time to note the sloping ground and thick shade before he pushed her, breasts first, against one of the vertical support pillars. He unfastened her cuffs, spun her so she faced him with her back pressing into the pillar, and re-secured her arms in front. His expression was neutral, and yet, she noted both darkness and determination.

If only she were on the ground she could run.

Before bringing her out here, he'd ordered her to stay the hell where she was. Then he'd gone downstairs and had returned carrying the familiar red rope, a slender whip, and a short glass of dark liquid. He'd taken those things onto the porch and had spent too much time out there doing things she hadn't been able to see, could only imagine.

Now he pulled her away from the pillar and under a rope he'd looped over a beam above her head. He tied one end of the rope to the chain between her wrists. That done, he took hold of the other end of the rope and walked with it to the railing. He pulled, and her arms lifted.

Up and up they went, reaching for nothing, forcing her to stretch as much as possible without standing on her toes. He secured his rope end to the railing and stepped away from it.

"Keeping you in place," he said unnecessarily.

It was late afternoon. The day was still warm but it would soon start to cool. Did he intend to keep her outside all night? If he did, she'd scream, take her chances that someone would hear. Maybe she should cry out now.

He stepped behind her, prompting her to look back at him. She shuddered when he picked up a length of rope from a small table near a substantial handmade wooden chair.

"You're going to listen to me for a while," he informed her as he doubled the rope. "Then, once I'm done, you're going to answer my questions."

There'd been no give to his voice, no hint that what she wanted meant anything to him. This was how things were going to be.

She didn't try to draw away when he placed two red strands in her mouth and tied them behind her head. The rope gag hadn't completely cut off her ability to make a sound, which maybe was what he intended.

After positioning her so she faced him, he sat in the chair he might have made and sipped his drink. After a few swallows, he put the glass down and picked up the whip. At the end were a half dozen thin leather strips.

"This" — he snapped the whip at her, the strips stinging her belly — "is to make sure I have your full attention. You weren't able to escape earlier because you're hardly the first woman I've taught the meaning of helplessness." He indicated his bad leg. "If it had been earlier in my recovery, you might have." Several lines of pain bloomed over her breasts.

"If you were a fully trained sex slave, you wouldn't have tried what you did." He again stung her breasts. "It wouldn't have occurred to you because you would have seen me and all men as your absolute Masters."

Sex slave.

He wasn't really hurting her. The strikes were like mosquito bites, quick to make their impact only to fade from her awareness. The awful thing was how he kept after her. She became a hooked fish being played with by a man in no hurry to end the battle. He occasionally stopped lashing her, and she imagined he was letting out enough

174

line so she could continue to fight. Then he started hitting her breasts, belly, and thighs again, reeling her in until his boat loomed over her.

And he talked.

Whether he was wielding the whip, sipping his drink, or just studying her, he continued his story. He'd been employed by Carnal Incorporated as a sex slave trainer for some ten years. At the beginning, he'd worked under the tutelage of men long accustomed to molding female minds and bodies, but even back then he'd been no novice. He didn't tell her why Carnal's management had initially taken him into their program, and of course, she couldn't ask.

Carnal was an international organization with training facilities located in the United States, primarily so top management could keep an eye on the operation. About half of the slaves came from this country, while the rest were flown in by well-paid private pilots. As a secret operation, Carnal paid no taxes. In more than twenty years of existence, it had never been investigated since the right palms had been, and continued to be, greased.

"Every time powerful, wealthy men place orders for a certain kind of woman, other trainers, or I go looking for one that meets our customer's demands. Locating a potential subject doesn't take long. What's time-consuming is determining how much risk is involved in grabbing her. Unless a woman is physically, socially, and emotionally isolated we won't bother with her." He leaned forward. "You met that criteria."

Was he saying she was already bought and paid for, that he'd taken her for profit and not his personal use?

"At present, there are five Carnal training facilities." He lashed one thigh then the other. "If I wanted to, I could take you to any of them. They're each unique, and yet they have a number of things in common. They're absolutely secure. No slave has ever escaped. The budget we trainers work with is generous. Within reason, we can order anything we believe will enhance the training experience. We're always experimenting."

Maybe he wanted her to think about what he meant by 'experimenting', but she couldn't, because he'd increased the whip's tempo. Dizzy from trying to twist away, she shook her head, trying to clear it. He concentrated on the outside of her left thigh, compelling her to turn her back to him. Then he switched to her buttocks.

He was spanking her, treating her like a misbehaving child.

Taking her into a place where — where what? Making her float.

"I've long been in favor of cages over other kinds of restraint. I often put a naked new capture in a four-by-four-foot enclosure. She can lie down but not stretch out. Whether she stands or sits is up to her. There's nothing but bars to look at, nothing except metal to touch. The lock is larger than it needs to be and makes its own impact. In time, I give her a bucket to pee in. She can drink but only by sucking out of the bottle I hold. If she wants to eat, she has to wait until I place the bites in her mouth. A few days of that, of seeing only me — it makes an impact."

Of course it did, maybe the same as what he was doing was changing her.

"Think about what's going on with you right now." He struck her ass, paused, teased her there again. "There aren't any cages here, no guards, no pictures or videos being sent to your eagerly waiting owner."

At first, it didn't register that he'd stopped detailing Carnal slave training and was talking about her again. She tried to pay close attention, to catch a warning before it was too late, but the attack on her buttocks was so intense.

Erotic.

Awash in another wave of helplessness, she faced him. The whip snapped an inch from her left nipple.

"I nearly lost it when you tried to hurt me," he said and leaned back again. He placed the whip on the floor within easy reach. "If it had been a few years ago — other trainers have had to pull me off slaves who made me angry."

He stood. She tensed and tried to move away, then stared after him as he headed into the bedroom. Something had happened to her mind and body that went beyond what he'd told her and done to her. Her existence revolved around this place, this man, the current spinning through her.

Master *knew* her, showed her a new way to be. To experience.

Maybe even to trust.

Was that possible?

He was both gone too long and back too soon — carrying the digital camera. "Rotate. I want to record this from all angles."

Not wanting to anger or disappoint him, she slowly did as he commanded. She was becoming Master's beast.

She didn't recoil from the thought but held it in front of her. With her arms over her head, she had to keep her legs together to lessen the strain throughout her body. As a result, her thighs were sealed together, her sex trapped and hot.

Needing more. Needing *him*.

At length, he'd recorded what he'd turned her into to his satisfaction. After draining his drink, he picked up the whip and walked around her, striking her as he did. The insect sting sensations landed everywhere, seemingly leaving no part of her untouched. Her breathing grew ragged.

Master's sex slave.

"Even if Carnal Incorporated is shut down, another will take its place," he said. "There will always be men with the means and desire to own human flesh." The whip clattered to the floor. "And because there are enough submissive women to feed that need. Some are converted from the independent women they were. Some, like you, come to it naturally."

With him behind her, she was hard-pressed to concentrate on what he'd just said.

"You smell of submission. It oozes from your pores."

She was still trying to find the lie in what he'd said when he reached around her. His too-large hand spread over her collar so the leather bit into her throat. There was nowhere to go, except into him. His chest rubbed her shoulders while his cock ground into the small of her back.

"One reason I often place a slave in a cage" — his other hand snaked around her hips — "is that way she isn't touched for a while. She has no doubt that sooner or later I'll start manhandling her. The waiting — the waiting helps break her down. You didn't need that."

He hadn't kept his hands off her. From the beginning, they'd roamed over her body, just as he was doing now.

If he asked what she was looking at, she wouldn't have been able to say, not with his strength sealing her to him, his hand heating the collar around her throat and his fingers between her legs.

Scared and excited, she surrendered to the primal need to give him as much access to her sex as possible. Even as she widened her stance, a part of her demanded an explanation. Didn't she have any pride? Any modesty?

Pride belonged to women with clothes and freedom of movement.

Women without submissive needs.

Master was no longer whipping her or taking her picture. He was fingering her because he knew how much she loved it.

Loved? Yes, that.

The pressure on her throat ended, and he worked on the knot that held her gag in place. The rope loosened, and she pushed it out of her mouth. He hadn't given her permission to talk.

"In time," he said, "you'll reveal everything about the thoughts, images, and needs that turn you on. I already know a great deal about them. Having your fantasy man be in charge touches you on a deep level. You don't know why, and that occasionally concerns you. As an independent woman, you should want to be a man's equal, so why do you envision yourself on your knees?"

Damn him, he was right.

The hand on her thighs had stilled while he'd been talking. When it started moving again, she squirmed but didn't try to break free. A muscled forearm pressed against her right breast, and he closed his fingers over her left, effortlessly trapping both. Claiming them — and her.

"Go back in your mind for me, slave," he muttered seductively. "Take me into your past and tell me about the events that formed the woman you turned into. Start with the parents you didn't want to talk about."

Caught off guard by his command, if that's what it was, she tried to separate herself from what he was doing to her body but couldn't. She was on Master's deck, in his chains and ropes, surrounded by him. Giving in to him.

"Why do you care?" she whispered around her tumbling thoughts. "Isn't...isn't controlling my body enough?"

He didn't immediately answer. "No, it isn't. Otherwise, I won't know if you're keeping things from me."

No, he wouldn't. But she'd held so much locked inside for so long, been so alone. "My parents are alcoholics," she blurted. "That says a lot, doesn't it?"

"They drank all the time you were growing up?"

She'd barely opened the window to the past and already his insight rocked her. The fingers on her sex stroked and caressed, while the hand over her breast cradled it. Surrendering to the living blanket around her, she rested her head against his chest.

"I, ah, I haven't seen them for a couple of years. The last time I did, the change in their appearance shocked me. They looked so old, wasted. They were living together then, but that could have changed. Again."

"So they sucked as parents. When did you leave home?"

Even though his question hadn't taken her into the most painful part of her life, strangely she wasn't ready to leave the subject of her childhood. Even as she tried to decide how much Master deserved to know, the strain on her up-thrust arms made it impossible for her to focus entirely on the gift of his body and hands. To take strength from him.

"A sensitive subject," he said. "I wondered how many I'd find. Let's try another approach. How did you lose your virginity?"

"What? With Mickey."

"Was the idea mutual?"

"Yes."

"How old were you?"

"Fifteen."

"That's fairly young. Did you know what you were getting into?"

"I, ah, my old man... I developed early and he, you know."

Master didn't press her to continue, and she silently thanked him. An all-knowing finger slipped past her clit hood and settled over the center of her ability to feel pleasure. Along with a shot of arousal, she felt...protected.

"My folks didn't care if my brothers and I saw them having sex so I had—"

"You thought you knew what sex was about."

"My old man talked about how I was turning into a cock tease. I wasn't sure what he was getting at. Then he tried to climb into my bed..."

"Tried? You weren't able to fight him off?"

Were they really having this conversation? Maybe the greater question was, what had he done to make her existence revolve around him?

Not taking time to judge the danger in what she was saying, she handed him the details of the nights her drunken father had tried to rape her. She wasn't sure how many times he'd waved his limp penis in her face, while straddling her before he'd given up. Disgusted as she'd been by the sight, she'd eventually stopped resisting. He'd rubbed himself all over her while she'd tried not to throw up, but he'd never been able to produce an erection. Finally, he'd told her it was her fault. No man would ever want such an ugly bitch.

The words 'ugly bitch' knotted her stomach. All those years later and they still hurt.

"Damn him," Master muttered. "Some men should never be fathers."

Was he speaking from personal experience? Would he ever reveal anything of his own past?

Please, I want to know.

"There's much more you're going to tell me, but I don't want to go at it like this anymore."

His tone made her wonder if he was confused, but that couldn't be. Master was in charge of everything that happened as witnessed by how effortlessly he'd kept her suspended between arousal and discomfort. He loosened the rope holding her arms up, and her belief in his take-charge personality took another forward step.

She couldn't help but groan as blood began to flow back through her arms. She didn't know what to do with them — or the rest of body. He was standing apart from her, just watching her, learning what about her?

Anxious and eager, she studied the rope dangling from her handcuffs.

Master's possession. Wearing his collar.

Rocked anew by the thoughts, she lifted her head. Master wasn't handsome. There were too many rough edges to him with dark whiskers blurring his jaw line. Too many scars.

And yet...

"Tell me something." He folded his arms. "How do you feel now that you told me about what your father tried to do?"

"Exhausted." But it was more than that. Even though the shadows had lengthened, she was still warm. She couldn't remember the last time she'd talked to someone else, let alone seen another human being. Master had become her world.

Master's gaze moved to her breasts. "Do they still sting?"

Despite the quick conversation change, she kept up.

She wasn't sure why she wanted to answer as honestly as possible, just that she did. "They feel alive."

He nodded and sat back in the chair. His leg probably ached. Would a massage help?

"Why do you think that is?" he asked.

The weariness she'd been struggling to overcome faded with every breath she took. Beyond all reason, there was something magical about these moments. She should've tried to figure out why that was, but just living in them was enough. She lifted her hands and cupped her breasts. Touching them reawakened the fluttering sensation in her pussy.

"Everything that's happened to me has been so intense."

"More or less than your old man trying to hump you?"

What would her sperm donor think if he could see her now? Would anyone recognize what she'd become? Did she? "They're nothing alike."

"Aren't they?" He waited a beat. "Two men have forced you against your will. Taken control of your life."

There was nothing casual about his comment. Maybe he intended to make her pay for saying the wrong thing, but she didn't think so.

Hoped not.

"I was a child then. Now I'm an adult."

"A naked and chained one who calls the man who did these things to her Master."

Her head pulsed so she could hardly think. She was on the brink of exhaustion with no way of knowing how her future would play out. She staggered over to the closest wall and leaned against it. Hopefully he wouldn't ask why she continued to cradle her breasts but why would he? He already knew.

He studied her for a long time, starting with her feet and slowly moving up her nude body. Something in his expression made her wonder if he was trying to decide to tell her something.

"You've never brought a captive here?" she ventured.

"No."

"Why did you with me?"

She expected him to point out that he'd been staying here since his accident and expediency had made the decision, but the longer he remained quiet, the less sure she became. His gaze was unsettling but far from how she'd felt every time her drunken father had stared at her. Back then she'd felt dirty. Now she had worth.

"What about the men in your life?" he asked unexpectedly. "Were those relationships influenced by what you had with your father?"

She looked past him to the darkening wilderness. Before long, night would further isolate her — and him — from the rest of the world.

"I just wanted to get away from my old man. Mickey —"

"Oh, yes, Mickey. The man who took your virginity."

Maybe someday she'd tell Master that his hard statements played a large role in what had broken her down. Now, however, she had all she could do to battle the sexual hunger warring with her weary body.

"What was the first time like?"

She pulled the memory around her. Eyes unfocused, she mentally returned to the afternoon Mickey had picked her up after school and driven her out to an abandoned barn he knew about. She hadn't wanted to go home because her parents had been drinking and fighting for days. Mickey had been twenty. In retrospect, she'd known he'd been too old for her, but back then he'd represented excitement, maturity, and security. They'd been doing some pretty heavy petting over the past few weeks, and the other night he'd taken off her bra and sucked on her breasts. Made her squirm.

She told Master that and more, even how Mickey had driven with his hand inside her pants. Once at the leaking wreck of a structure, he'd shown her the sleeping bag he'd spread out over some hay he'd raked together. She'd shaken as he'd undressed her and averted her eyes while he'd stretched a condom over his erection.

A voice she barely recognized told Master how she'd still been asking herself if this was what she wanted to do when Mickey had laid her out on the sleeping bag and crawled on top of her.

"It hurt, but it was over so fast I barely knew what was happening."

"Hair trigger. It goes with being young." Master patted the broad chair arm. "Come here."

Trembling much as she'd done that first day with Mickey, she walked over to where Master was sitting and perched on the chair. He pulled her around toward him, lifted her legs onto his lap, and rested his hand on her thigh. She couldn't relax. Maybe she didn't want to.

"What about the next time?"

Chapter Fourteen

Master was touching her. Connecting with her. How could she be anything except honest? As the shadows deepened, she painted a picture of the weeks and months following their first time. Mickey had been insatiable when it had come to sex. The longer they'd been together, the more she'd wanted the same thing. Mickey had known what triggers to touch and what to say to make her feel like a woman. She had barely been able to concentrate on her classes since at the end of the day her boyfriend would be waiting for her. She'd climb into his car, spread her legs, and throw back her head. Beg to be fucked.

Mickey had called her his whore. Far from being embarrassed, she'd taken the word as a badge of honor. Proof that someone loved her.

"He knew how awful things were for me at home. One day I couldn't talk for crying. I don't remember what had happened, probably more of the same. Anyway, Mickey said we should live together."

"Were you still fifteen?"

"Yes. I know what you're going to say, that I was too young."

"You were."

Up to now every time Master touched her it had been to hurt or sexually stimulate her. His large hand on her thigh served as a reminder of both what he was capable of and something deeper. Something she needed.

A mechanic, Mickey had lived in an apartment over a closed-up furniture store. That part of town was in sad shape, but she hadn't told Mickey how much it had spooked her to be there alone. Anything had been better than being around her parents. Used to living hand to mouth, she hadn't asked Mickey for anything.

Looking back, she realized the school had known how little money the family had, since she'd gotten free lunches in exchange for helping to clean the cafeteria afterward. Once she'd moved in with Mickey, she'd started bringing home leftovers. Mickey had kept saying their money problems were temporary and his boss intended to make him a partner once he'd learned more about the business.

But that had never happened and some weeks Mickey had barely made enough to pay the rent. Sex had continued to be incredible — once she'd had her first climax she hadn't been able to get enough. Maybe, she told Master, that's why Mickey and she had stayed together. That and her ability to supply them with almost everything they ate. Also, come summer, Mickey had hoped to earn what he'd called a shitload of money fighting forest fires. Shortly before school had let out, she'd gone everywhere she'd been able to think of looking for work. She hadn't told Mickey what she'd been doing, in part because she hadn't been sure she'd been going about it the right way, in part because what if she'd failed? It hadn't been as if she'd had a lot of self-confidence.

A place selling Chinese food at the mall food court had hired her to work fifteen hours a week, most of them evenings and weekends. She'd been proud of her accomplishment, but Mickey had complained that he hardly ever saw her.

"You two were fighting?" Master asked.

He'd been quiet for so long that his question caught her off guard. The wood under her buttocks was hard, and her shoulders were getting cold. His hand still rested on her thigh, keeping it warm.

"I didn't say anything when he raged on me. I didn't want to be like Mom, screaming all the time."

"He should have given you credit for bringing in some money."

Why Master had taken her side didn't matter as much

as realizing how much she was revealing. Now that she'd begun, she couldn't stop. By the middle of August, Mickey had only been called out to fight one fire. Even though the worst fires usually occurred in late summer and early fall when the forests were dry, he'd been getting more and more uptight. Then one day soon after she'd gotten her driver's license, he'd suggested they go for a ride in the mountains. She'd been so glad to see him in an upbeat mood that she'd hurried to pack a picnic lunch.

"He let me drive. He'd taught me how to drive, but this was the first time I'd been off paved roads. I was nervous because I didn't want to cause any damage to his car. He, ah, he talked about wouldn't it be something if someone started a fire out here. That way he'd get a lot of work at great pay."

"He was that someone?"

She wanted to jump to her feet and hide, but it was too late so she nodded and wrapped her hands around her arms. Today was surreal. Everything that had happened to her lately seemed more dream than reality.

"I didn't know it, but he'd put a gas can in the trunk. After we'd gone about twenty miles on this old logging road, he told me to stop."

"You could have grabbed the can once you realized what he was up to."

"I should have but I didn't. He was five years older than me, and I was hesitant because things hadn't been good between us lately. Also…"

"Also what?"

"We needed the money," she whispered, then went on to describe how Mickey had poured gas over the dried grasses and bushes. The moment he'd touched a lighter to them, everything had exploded. She'd jumped back in the car and was turning around while Mickey had thrown the gas can into the fire. They'd argued all the way back, with her telling him the fire would kill animals and birds and him saying she should have stopped him long ago.

By the next morning, Mickey had been called to fight the fast-moving fire, leaving her to listen to the news stories about how arson was suspected. A day later, the police had knocked on the door. Unknown to them, a fire lookout had spotted their vehicle. Her fingerprints were on the steering wheel so she couldn't deny she'd been driving.

"Mickey got a friend to testify he'd been with him, and I set the fire. Mickey kept saying he had no idea I was so worried about finances that I'd do something so crazy."

"They believed him?"

"They couldn't prove otherwise," she managed. Time had blunted a lot of the pain she'd experienced at the realization that the man she'd loved had turned on her, but telling Master brought so much back.

"Did you tell them the truth?"

Fighting the need for his arms around her, she shook her head. "I couldn't speak. I just sat there while detectives accused me of doing millions of dollars' worth of damage. I was a minor so my name didn't make the news, but the cops told my parents. They finally came to see me, and I knew they believed I was guilty. They blamed...they blamed me for getting hooked up with a loser, said I got what I deserved."

Irrational as it was, she kept hoping Master would say something in her defense, but all he did was start to stand up. She jumped to her feet. His features contorted as he put his weight on his bad leg.

"Master? Is there something I can —?"

He grabbed her arm and turned her so she faced the door to the bedroom. "You've already done enough. We're going inside."

Some of the tightness in his leg had eased by the time Reno and his slave-in-training were back in the bedroom. It was his own damn fault for sitting so long. He'd probably given her the impression he held her responsible, but the truth was listening to her had taken him out of himself.

He was tempted to thank her for giving him a break from self-absorption, not that he would, would he? He needed to focus on getting her to tell him the rest of what had happened after she'd been accused of starting a fire.

Looking at her as she stood with her manacled hands against her naked belly, he couldn't connect what she was today with the teenager she'd once been. His guess was that girl had crawled into an emotional shell after her boyfriend and parents had deserted her. In contrast, this woman — yes, woman — was now comfortable in her own skin. The training he'd imposed on her hadn't broken her. She was stronger — and at peace with the submissiveness she maybe hadn't realized lived within her.

For the first time since he'd learned what it meant for one human to own another, he cared about what went on inside a slave's head and heart.

He didn't question what he was doing, just unlocked her cuffs and placed them and the rope still tied to them on the bed. Slave training had accustomed him to living with a nearly perpetual hard-on, but this was different, more personal. He wanted to fuck her, but it should be her idea as much as his.

Surprised by the thought, he continued to study her. Except for the collar, she wore nothing. The whip marks had faded so he could barely see them in the dim lighting, but no doubt their impact remained in his slave's psyche. Thinking of a slave as his was so new he couldn't quite wrap his mind around it. One thing he did know — he was horny.

And vulnerable.

Hell no!

Determined to separate himself from the unwanted thought, he drew his shirt over his head and kicked off the slippers he'd taken to wearing after the accident. He reached for his jeans fastening.

She sank to her knees. "Master, please let me."

Interesting. Not long ago, she'd talked almost as if they

were equals, but she'd slipped back into her new role without encouragement.

"Go on," he said. "And while you're doing it, tell me about your trial and its outcome."

She licked her lips but didn't speak until she was pulling down on his zipper. "It wasn't a regular trial thanks to my age. I was assigned a lawyer who told me to plead guilty. I didn't care."

It had been so damn easy for her to kneel that he had to work at not resenting her for it.

"You didn't get decent representation," he said, hoping to distract himself from her presence. "You should have implicated Mickey, made him pay for what he did."

She guided his jeans down his hips. "I know that now, but it's over. I can't relive the past."

"No one can." He balanced himself by planting his hand on her head while she dragged the jeans over his feet.

She rocked back on her heels. Arousal radiated out from every inch of her young body. His too. Much as she wanted to touch him, she was waiting for permission. Keeping his own needs under wraps was harder than he remembered. Reminding himself that he'd spilled himself in her mouth not long ago didn't help.

"Master? Can I ask a question?"

No slave had ever said that to him, but then, he'd never had any indication they'd cared about him as a human being. To them, he'd been a powerful force over which they'd had no control.

"Go ahead. I'll decide whether I want to answer."

She ducked her head in acceptance and rubbed her thighs as if trying to give herself courage. Imagining her locked up for so much of her teen years tightened his belly. Maybe the lengthy incarceration had stripped her of essential self-determination, but he was more inclined to believe her submissive nature went deeper.

Perhaps the once unwanted child had spent her life looking for someone to give her a sense of belonging.

Thinking through the possibility so distracted him that he had to ask her to repeat herself.

"What made you want to dominate?" she asked.

Don't answer. Tell her it's none of her damn business. "It got me off the streets, and, once I got good at it, the money was fantastic."

"Off the streets?"

He wasn't ready to tell her about choosing homelessness over living with his abusive stepfather at the age she'd been when she'd been incarcerated, or Fred, the bar owner who'd given him a roof over his head in exchange for working as a bouncer. Neither did he have any desire to spell out how he'd gone from dealing with drunks to becoming an apprentice slave trainer in what had turned out to be Fred's real business. Maybe he would someday. Truth was, despite the protective layers the telling would strip away, he didn't put it out of the realm of possibility. Now, however, was, in part, about putting an end to the pounding in his cock.

As for the other part— "Everyone is formed in large part by their upbringing. I don't have to tell you that. Let's just say, it only took having to use my fists once to realize it beat the hell out of the alternative, which I knew too damn much about. Maybe things would have turned out different for you if you'd punched out Mickey or your old man."

She lifted her hands and rotated them. "I could never…"

"Did you ever want to?"

She frowned. "If I did, I don't remember it. My mother — Dad called her a bitch. I can't imagine being like her."

"What do you want to do with your hands?"

"Use them to give you pleasure."

No slave had ever— "Why?"

Her eyes closed, and she rocked back and forth. "I don't know. When you grabbed me I was terrified you were going to kill me, at least rape me." Her lashes fluttered, then she was staring at him again. "Why didn't you?"

Much as he needed to fuck her, he was glad he was still wearing his briefs since sometimes talking accomplished more than action. As for whether this was one of those times, he could only go with instinct, which was something he almost never depended on. That was why he was a successful slave trainer. He had the steps and routine down to a science.

Routine and lessons be damned.

"Most of my co-workers start ramming their cocks into pussies from the first day, but I get more mileage out of making a subject anticipate."

The faintest smile touched the corners of her mouth. "Do you tell them what you're doing?"

"Of course not," he admitted, even though he sensed where the conversation was heading — into dangerous-for-him territory.

Still barely smiling, she brushed her fingertips over his thighs. "Do you let trainees do this?"

Delicious tension seized him. "Hell no."

"But you are today, because I'm different."

It wasn't a question, and even if it had been, he had no intention of answering. It seemed as if they'd been talking for hours, peeling off layers after all. In many respects, he didn't yet know her any more than she did him, but he'd already gone so damn deep. It wasn't that he'd said so much. However, now that he'd started pulling the real him out of the shadows, he wanted to continue.

Needed to.

Just as he suspected she had done.

"I want to be here." She leaned forward. Her head rested against his groin. Her soft fingers snaked around his hips. "Pleasing you."

How long ago had a woman last willingly touched him? Damn it, why hadn't he gone in search of normal relationships with members of the opposite sex? Much as he wanted to tell himself it was because the job was all-consuming, he knew that wasn't it. He dominated women. He didn't see one as an equal. As for her —

"What's your name?"

She blinked. "Kaci," she muttered, still clinging to him with his erection caught between them.

Kaci. Slave and more.

"We're going to have sex." *Maybe for starters, if I can take that step.*

"Yes, Master."

"Master Reno."

Eyes brimming, she nodded.

Chapter Fifteen

After Master Reno had put the collar on her, she'd felt trapped by it. Now she wondered if she might willingly wear it for the rest of her life. At the moment, he was using the ring at her throat to guide her over to the bed.

"Our relationship won't be like any you've ever had," he said.

For you, either?

Much as she wanted to know everything about his relationships with women, she didn't ask. A great deal had changed between them today and yet they were far from equals.

"Get onto the bed. Turn your back to me. Get onto your knees. Lean over," he ordered.

Lowering her arms and head to the mattress, she quivered in anticipation. Did he intend to take her in the ass? Mouth dry, she looked back in time to see him yank off his shorts.

"It's time for you to understand something—and for me, too. We're on a journey. I set the rules. I'll also be sensitive to the messages you give out." His expression sober, he planted his hands on her buttocks. "I've learned self-control. For us to be on the same journey, you need to learn to be patient as well, to wait."

"Wait?" Her pussy was so wet.

"Pleasure and pain. Building on the link between us."

"Are you're going to hurt me again, Master?"

"Not now."

"But maybe later?"

"I haven't decided."

She sensed pressure against her sex. Sighing, she pushed

back.

"Not yet." He lightly slapped her ass cheeks. "Draw out the anticipation."

I want to.

His hands deserted her buttocks and began traveling along her sides toward her breasts. She drew her arms down from over her head in preparation for pushing her upper body off the bed to give him access.

"Don't. I haven't given you permission to move."

"I'm sorry, Master." Master. She didn't dare ever forget what he was to her. What she wanted him to remain.

Before she could put her arms back where they'd been, he took hold of her wrists and eased her arms behind her. Then he pulled her up so her upper body was off the bed and her breasts dangled. His cock slipped past her slick entrance.

Full. Master inside me. Making us one.

"Damn you." His breath hissed.

"Damn me?"

"Be quiet. You've always fought your submissive nature." He pushed deeper, breathed hard. "You sure as hell didn't want your parents to know so they could take advantage of it. Anyone watching you handle your life will believe you're determined to be in charge. I know the truth."

The hot strain in her arms wasn't enough to distract her from him or his words. Hunger bloomed.

"Tell me about the desires you keep to yourself. Now. Before we — I'll know whether you're being truthful. If you lie" — he thrust into her, only to retreat — "you won't get what you need."

Neither would he, but he didn't seem to mind. Undoubtedly this lesson was part of his plan to bring out what he wanted from her.

What she needed to be.

"When it's just you, a solitary night and the truth, where do your thoughts take you?"

She could do this for Master. Wanted to. "I'm a sex slave.

Master keeps me in a…a cage."

"Does he? You aren't afraid of being locked up or kept in small spaces?"

He lowered her back onto the bed and released her arms. Blood flowed through them as she positioned them over her head. She wished he'd take her hands. Make her his.

"Maybe that's why I make up the scenes I do," she admitted. *Be honest about everything.* "I'm not constrained by reality."

"What is this Master of yours like?"

Keep going. Let it all out. "Harsh. Often cruel. He doesn't care about me as a human being, just that I do as he commands." She swallowed. "That I suffer for him."

"He beats you?" His cock just touching her sex, Master Reno massaged her buttocks.

Please, don't stop. Go deeper. Fuck me. Let me — "Yes. Sometimes he gets carried away. Anger—he has a great deal of anger in him."

"Do you know why?"

"No." She paused. "I know almost nothing about him."

His fingers kissed her ass, her thigh, her pelvis. "That way, it's easier to manipulate him to play the role you've assigned him."

Maybe he was right. In fact, she only had a hazy notion of what her make-believe Master looked like. As long as he was bigger, stronger, and in control, that was enough.

"Go on."

The words were barely out of his mouth when he drew her labia lips apart and eased his erection deep into her. Whimpering, she struggled not to push against him, to obey.

"He keeps me in chains. I wear a collar."

"Like the one I put on you?"

Your gift to me. "No, thicker and heavier. There are metal cuffs around my wrists and ankles. I can't find a way to remove them."

"You need this Master to be in total control."

Once, after she'd had too much to drink, she'd pictured herself going to a psychiatrist and telling her all about her fantasies. The shrink, a prim older woman, had fainted.

"I didn't think about his motives." Being half-fucked was so damn distracting. Wonderful. Too much. "All that registered was how he made me feel. The restraints—I guess I was thinking I'd spend the rest of my life wearing them."

"Being restrained and controlled satisfies a need for you." He shoved into her. "There's more than one kind of confinement."

For several moments, she couldn't begin to wrap her splintered mind around what he'd said. Maybe—maybe he was talking about how his life had been impacted by his accident. Of course, it had been. He'd gone from shaping captives' lives to what—trying to crawl out from under a wrecked motorcycle?

Did he have nightmares? Need a way to escape them?

"All right," he said after a short silence, "back to—what does this Master do to marry pain to pleasure for you?"

"Beatings," she whispered. *Will you let me into your mind and heart? Be as honest as I'm being?* "Nipple clamps."

"Which do you prefer?"

She tried to pull up details of the scenarios she'd created and embellished, but it was so hard. Master Reno was fucking her. Giving her this much of himself.

"The clamps," she finally thought to say.

"Why?"

How many questions did he intend to ask? Did his ability to deny himself sexual release have no end?

"I-I don't know, Master."

"Think." He punctuated his command by slapping her buttocks.

Distracted by the delicious sensation, she wiggled her ass at him. He chuckled then tightened his hold on her buttocks.

"Why clamps over whips?"

"The way they look, I guess." This was insane. How could

they be carrying on a conversation?

"What do you think when you look at your breasts and see metal clamped to your nipples?"

"I—trapped."

"What else?"

"Excited."

"Like you are right now?"

My honesty, followed by yours? "It's as if there are two sides to me, the part I understand and is turned on by, you know, normal things."

"Like this?"

He eased his cock into her, slowly spreading sensitive tissues and turning them from two to one. She loved the deep connection. Fed from it.

"Yes," she hissed. "Yes, like this. Oh, thank you, Master."

He stayed tight against her. "What about your other side?" His voice sounded strained. "What turns you on about imagining having clamps placed on your breasts?"

Think. Give him what he deserves. "It, ah, comes from knowing I have no control or responsibility. Master can do whatever he wants to me, but he won't damage me. He knows how far to go."

"Do you trust him?"

Master Reno had sealed himself to her and that was robbing her of her intellect. Maybe he could think while fucking, but she couldn't. Didn't want to try.

"I trust you."

He pulled back, only to hurl himself at her so she slid forward. He grabbed her hips and drew her against him. "Are you afraid?"

"Overwhelmed. Master, you overwhelm me."

"I hope I always do."

Much as she needed to ask him about 'always', that could wait. Panting, she spread her legs and dug her toes into the spread. He again withdrew, only to spear her so forcefully he nearly knocked her onto her belly. She debated suggesting he take hold of her arms again to keep her in place, but a slave didn't tell a Master how to fuck.

"Damn," he said and withdrew.

Feeling lost, she took a chance on rolling onto her side. His erection was wet with her juices and her pussy quivered.

"On your back."

As she complied, awareness of her collar became nearly as powerful as her readiness for sex. He climbed onto the bed and settled himself on his knees. He drew her toward him so the backs of her thighs rested on the fronts of his with her bent legs behind him. She took care to keep her weight off his left leg. After running his nails from between her breasts clear to her mons and making her squeal, he rose and hauled her even closer. Sweet pressure against her pussy had her lifting her buttocks in an attempt to increase the alignment.

Cock inside pussy. Completing her.

Thinking to mirror what he'd done, she aimed her nails at his chest. He shook his head. "Not this time, slave. I do. I control. You experience."

He eased his hands under her buttocks and began thrusting. The attack consumed her. She ran her fingers into her hair and closed her eyes. In her mind, Master Reno loomed over her, watching her breasts jiggle and listening to her harsh breathing. She should do the same, but these were deeply personal and vulnerable moments for a man.

This was her Master, as mysterious as he was powerful. Better to dive into the images that had sustained her through all those lonely nights.

Attacking his helpless captive, listening to her squeal, laughing at her futile attempts to break free of overwhelming and unending arousal. Showing no mercy, pushing her onward and onward until only release was important.

Denying her.

Fantasy died. In its place came the realization that Master Reno cared as much about her pleasure as his own. Otherwise, he wouldn't have taken hold of her nipples, making her think of metal clamps.

"Feel," he said softly. "Take the sensations into you." His hold on her hard nubs tightened. "Let pleasure and pain melt together."

What pain? Arousal spread over her. Nothing existed beyond hot hunger. Master's potent body hammered at hers. His cock abraded her inner walls and they wept. She opened her eyes, saw him, nothing but him.

Felt him. Rode with him.

Her climax struck. She was charging unprotected into a storm. Hot wind and driving rain pummeled her, sent her flying.

He came with a series of jerks that held her hard against her own release and kept it going. Sweat burst from her pores to join with his. For a few seconds, they were equals.

Then, finished, Master released her nipples and raked his nails over and down her body. Moaning, crying in delight, she let Master do as he wished with her.

* * * *

"I've never hunted."

"I'm glad to hear that, but why not? Being surrounded by the wilderness the way you are, it would be easy."

Reno glanced up from whatever he'd been reading on his cell phone. "Is that something you think I should be doing? Bastard of a sex slave trainer blasts away at everything that moves?"

"No," she hurried to say. She stood in the kitchen stir-frying the vegetables she'd found in his refrigerator. Even though she had on one of his T-shirts, his look stripped her. "I didn't mean that. I'm just..."

"Trying to learn more about me?"

"Yes, Master."

He nodded. "Why?"

The easy way out would be to stumble through a non-response, but they both deserved better. Less than an hour ago they'd climaxed at nearly the same time and now, even though he'd said he wanted to see if she could cook, something was coming to life between them.

"That can't surprise you," she said. "You're fascinating. Complex."

He frowned.

"You don't want to be." She hurried her words. "You've always kept your slave trainees at arm's length."

After a glance at his phone, he again regarded her. "My job calls for me turning a trainee inside out, not the other way around."

"I know." She felt, not sorry for him, but much as she had while she was locked-up. No one had cared about the confused and hurt girl with worthless parents and a boyfriend who'd lied and deserted her. Day by day, she'd built a wall around her emotions. Maybe her coping techniques had manifested themselves in her need to turn her very existence over to a Master. "How did you wind up working for Carnal Incorporated?"

He didn't answer. Neither did he order her to stop asking questions. She still wore his collar and whatever he told her to do, she would. Their relationship was complex. Hopefully it would always be like that.

Always?

"I shouldn't have asked, Master. I had no right."

"Maybe. Maybe not. That smells good."

"I told you I can cook."

"Then I'll keep you."

The words hung between them. If he kept her, he'd want more than a cook.

A sex slave.

Someone to talk to.

To be part of.

"There."

Pulled out of herself, she realized he was indicating at the phone. "What is it, Master?"

"Damek just got back to me. He wants us to work together."

"Doing what?" *Will you leave me?*

Instead of reminding her, as he had every right to, that she had no business asking questions, he read what Damek had texted.

"'Hell yes, I want you. Why do you think I kept talking about the business? If you're sure you're ready to adjust and adapt your technique, how soon can you get your ass here?'"

Unable to concentrate on anything except the ramifications of those words, she turned off the stove and walked over to Master Reno. He was sitting on one side of the counter while she stood opposite him. Marks still circled her wrists and heat from the stove was making the whip marks itch.

"Damek and I have worked together for years. We sometimes clashed but haven't for a long time. He's as much of a bastard as I am."

She covered his hands with hers. His warmth and life slipped into her, prompting her to press her thighs together. To anticipate. "You aren't a bastard."

"Aren't I? Don't forget what I did to you."

"I loved it."

His stare went on and on. "I know you did. We're both fucked-up."

"Maybe."

"No 'maybe' to it."

Unwilling to argue, she waited for him to continue. The log walls, stone fireplace, exquisite staircase, and handmade furniture said a great deal about the man who lived here.

"Damek and I will no longer be working for Carnal. We're going to open our own operation."

Doing what? She didn't ask since Master might be displeased and she needed to please him. To fuck him.

He drew his hands out from under hers and captured her wrists. "There are a lot of women like you. They want the world to see them as standing on their own two feet, but when they're behind closed doors with—"

"With their Masters?"

"If they have one. Thousands are looking for someone to belong to. They need to be trained so those someone will want them. That's what Damek and I'll be doing."

Master would be touching other women, putting them through what he'd put her through? Jealousy and loss closed her eyes.

"I know what you're thinking, slave." He squeezed her wrists. "But you're wrong."

"I am?"

"Yes. Open your eyes."

She obeyed. No, he wasn't handsome, but she didn't want him to be. Everything about him spoke to her, even the scars she now believed he'd tell her about. Some day — or night — he'd let her into his past just as she'd done.

"Those women will be clients. You're mine. It's what we both need." He released one wrist and stroked her collar. "The one I'll lock around your neck will be red. A combination of leather and metal."

Her legs threatened to go out from under her. "With your name on it so everyone will know I belong to you."

"Yes," he muttered and indicated that she was to come around the counter.

She waited until he'd pulled her back against his chest and his hands covered her breasts. "Thank you, Master."

Naked Nights

Excerpt

Chapter One

"She won't stand a chance against you, not with you weighing so much more than she does."

Tray Nix didn't need to be told that. After all, he'd yet to come across a woman who could hold her own against him. The same could be said for ninety-nine percent of the male population. Even though his pro football years were behind him, he still competed in weightlifting events. Just the width of his shoulders was enough to convince most people not to confront him.

"I can see why they arranged to have Carnal harvest her," his companion continued as they waited for the next Copper County race to begin. "The bitch is making fools of the male jockeys here."

By 'they', Carnal Incorporated executive Robert Smith was referring to several heavy betters who couldn't bring themselves to back a female jockey. To them, horse racing was a boys' club. Women could sit in the stands like he and Robert were doing. They could even own horses and work as trainers. However, pitting their racing skills against men, even if the men barely topped one hundred pounds, went against everything their betters believed in.

"They should lay down money on her," Tray suggested. "Seems to me that would end what they consider a problem and turn it into an asset."

Robert chuckled, not that anyone who didn't know the expensively dressed fifty-something man would call it a chuckle. To an outsider, the sound probably came across as a warning, Robert's way of saying he didn't give a damn about anyone's opinion.

The thing was, Tray didn't give a damn what Robert thought and Robert knew it. Their relationship was both complex and simple, two men with very little in common who nevertheless had agreed to work together.

Work? That was one way of putting it.

"I wagered a grand on her." Robert had to press his shoulder against Tray's so they could carry out a private conversation in the crowded stands. "What about you?"

Damn it, betting that much on a weekday ten-furlong race held in a rural county would stand out. Robert had gotten rich too fast helping run Carnal and had lost perspective. If they were going to pull off the harvesting, they had to keep a low profile — at least as low a profile as Tray was capable of. No matter that he was casually dressed in jeans and blue T-shirt, he stood out. He always did.

The eight thoroughbreds in this race were being loaded into the starting gates. From this distance, the animals didn't look that imposing, but he'd been around enough horses to have a healthy respect for them, especially high strung ones. No way would he be on the back of a twelve-hundred-pound beast hellbent on galloping as hard as its heart allowed, especially with other straining beasts all around.

He and Robert had come to Copper County to harvest Marina Stenson, but he'd insisted on observing her in her natural habitat. It wasn't that he gave a damn about the woman herself—years of being a broad-magnet tended to make them all blur together—but her choice of jobs fascinated him.

Some five minutes ago, he'd been standing near the paddock area watching the horses being mounted. Because the jockeys had all worn helmets, at first he hadn't been able to make her out. Then one had turned sideways, giving him a glimpse of breasts under red and black silks. He'd thought the male jockeys might shun her, but they hadn't. Interesting.

She'd hoisted herself onto the back of a chestnut mare, picked up the reins, and leaned over the mare's neck to scratch her between the ears. Watching Marina, he'd wondered what her hands would feel like on him.

Hell, that wasn't what today was about. In time, if things played out the way they were supposed to, she'd learn to accept his hands all over her. Maybe move from tolerating to—

The horses exploded from the starting gate, hooves pounding the packed earth. This was a far cry from the Kentucky Derby, but the crowd's excitement was contagious. Silent, he leaned forward, his gaze locked on the blur of red and black now in second place. Marina's mount ran as if she was trying to beat the ground into submission. Despite that, Marina seemed part of the animal under her, quiet water surrounded by raging rapids. Thanks to his familiarity with horses, it didn't take him long to pick up on a key reason for her success. No matter what was happening around her, Marina remained calm, and that calmness reached her horse. The mare stopped attacking the turf. Her strides lengthened and became smooth. Two furlongs from the end, the duo flowed past the lead horse and cruised to an easy win.

"Damn!" Robert exclaimed. "That's the easiest money

I've made all year."

The horses cantered around the track as their riders brought them down from the highs they'd been on. Marina's mare still reminded him of moving water, while Marina now sat straight and proud, looking all around. He could see why someone who hadn't bet on her might see her stance as arrogance. What he didn't understand was how anyone could hate her enough to arrange to have her freedom taken away.

What did he care? By the end of the day, he'd start training Marina Stenson as a sex slave. She'd either be put up for auction at the end or sold before he'd finished working with her. Chances were she'd never sit on horseback again.

Hell, he knew what facing the end of something he loved felt like.

* * * *

Maybe she should have accepted Barker's invitation to buy her a beer, Marina thought as she pulled into the carport next to her small house. After all, Barker had been the first to give her a chance to race and she didn't like thinking about where she'd be without him. Unfortunately, sixty-eight-year-old Barker smelled worse than the fairground's stables. He was also getting hard of hearing and spoke so loudly he gave her a headache. Her other option had been to join several of the jockeys, which was a pretty safe bet because she'd seldom seen one drink more than a single beer. However, by the time she'd gotten away from a reporter, almost everyone had taken off.

The interview questions had been predictable. How did she feel about being a woman in a male-dominated sport? Why had she decided to become a jockey? Was she ever afraid? What did she intend to do once her riding years were over?

She'd had no hesitancy about answering the first two questions but the others were no one's business. Of course fear occasionally factored in, but so far she'd been able to transfer the emotion into determination and split-second decisions. As for her plans for the rest of her life — she had them all right. What she needed was a bankroll to make them come true, which was why she was living in what was little more than a cabin on the five acres she'd bought at auction. All the acreage needed was a water source and fencing to become useful but —

"Enough," she muttered and unlocked the front door. Her fingers still tingled from gripping the reins during the three races she'd ridden in today and her inner thighs ached from holding on. Fortunately, she'd recently put in a new hot water heater and she intended to stand in the shower until it ran out.

Because she needed to check the oil level in her truck, she didn't bother locking the door before tugging off her racing boots. The house was too quiet, eerily empty. Until a month ago she'd shared it with Zero, the mutt she'd found along the side of the road the week she'd turned eighteen. After Zero had died in her arms, she'd stroked his gray muzzle for hours then buried him in the shade of an oak tree. At first she'd been too heartbroken to contemplate having another dog. Then she'd decided that the best way to honor her companion's memory was by giving another stray a home. Unless something came up, she planned to go to the humane society on Wednesday and adopt another mutt.

Smiling, she drew her top over her head and unfastened the confining sports bra on her way to her bedroom. She dropped her discarded clothes on the floor, took a ratty but clean T-shirt and shorts out of her dresser, and entered the bathroom with what she intended to wear after her shower. She leaned against the sink so she could tackle her leggings and the tight breeches that came to just below her knees. That left her with lacy white underwear, her only concession to her feminine side — except for the long, mostly black hair she wrestled into braids on race days. After shimmying out of the bikini, she turned on the water. While waiting for the room to steam, she unbraided her hair and shook her head. *Ah, freedom!*

Yeah, freedom, she acknowledged as she stepped into the small shower. Responsible for nothing and no one except herself and her future dog. Independent. Self-sufficient.

Pitting herself and her mount against the opposition, with her muscles straining and adrenaline flowing, left her more exhilarated at a race's end than before the start. It took hours to come down off the incredible and nerve-wracking high, which meant she'd be wired until long after dark. Even hot water flowing over her did little to quiet the familiar jumpiness, not that she wanted it any other way.

Hell, she wasn't getting any sex these days and frustration contributed to the jumpiness. Fortunately, she knew how to take care of that. Eyes closed, she leaned her back against the shower wall, spread her legs, and slipped her right hand over what her father had called her woman's place. She flicked one nipple then the other, awakening her breasts. Poor Dad. He'd done an admirable job as a single parent right up until his little girl had started to mature sexually. That was when he'd started stammering and shoving sex education books at her.

Maybe they would have gotten past the awkward stage. She'd certainly hoped and expected that would have happened. However, Dad had died shortly before her fifteenth birthday.

No! No thinking about that tonight! She'd made five hundred dollars today. The evening was hers—time for a little self-satisfaction.

One caress. Two. Three. Then more and more strokes along her labia until her knees weakened and hot juices drenched her fingers. Her head fell back, her mouth opened and her nostrils flared. She switched from teasing her taut nipples to pinching them. Pain and something damn good radiated over her size C breasts. Sensation flowed down her middle and met with the sweet energy encompassing her sex.

Well versed in her hot buttons, she conjured up a naked male body. Unlike the men she'd spent her day competing against, the one residing in her mind was heavily muscled with impossibly wide shoulders. Tall and self-confident, he invaded her space and pulled her hands off her body. He made her stand with her arms at her sides as he slipped two fingers past her parted lips. He didn't speak, simply commanded her with a dark look. Even though she wasn't sure she could trust her legs, she remained where he'd ordered and started mouth-fucking his fingers. She repeatedly licked him while staring up into his hooded eyes. The drawing sensation radiated down her neck, spread over her breasts and began a familiar trail to her pussy.

Do what I command you to, his gaze said. Give me access to all your holes.

A calloused palm pressed against her mons. Desperate for more, she arched her pelvis toward him. He grunted and shoved more firmly. When she stood her ground, when she opened herself even more to him, he nodded. Fingers closed over her labia, making her moan in anticipation.

Then the intimate invasion shifted, the texture changed, and she reluctantly acknowledged it was just herself after all. She remained with her legs far apart as she withdrew her wet fingers from her mouth and stroked her breasts. The feminine fingers between her legs invaded then filled her opening. It wasn't what she wanted, her fingers were too small, but she'd make do. Fuck herself as the water cooled.

She came, a feathery climax that made her skin burn, followed by lethargy. Feeling both satisfied and still frustrated, she aimed the water at her pussy and washed away the scant discharge. Hopefully she'd be able to sleep. If not, there were always her sex toys.

By the time she'd dried herself, put on shirt and shorts without bothering with underwear and wrapped a towel around her head, she'd mostly convinced herself that she was crazy for thinking she could achieve a teeth-rattling climax on her own. At least it hadn't taken long. Once she'd dried her hair and found her sandals, she'd tend to her truck, starting with adding some oil. While she was at it, she should check the antifreeze and windshield fluid levels. Then, glory be, she'd rustle up something to eat.

The bedroom she'd just stepped into smelled — off. Different. Confused and a little uneasy, she stopped and looked around. Two men stood in the opening between her bedroom and living room. One was huge, an unbelievable mix of height and strength. The other barely registered.

"What the hell are you doing here?" she demanded.

Neither man spoke. Her heart slammed against her chest as if trying to break free. At the same time, her thoughts slowed, focused on the only thing that mattered — survival.

"Leave. Get out of my place."

They continued staring at her. Granted, the window was open enough that she could dive through it but she'd take the screen with her. Adding to the risk, she was barefoot.

She wanted to demand an explanation but didn't because she wouldn't like their response. This was bad, on the brink of a nightmare. If she was going to get out of right now alive, she had to do something.

Not taking her attention off them, she stepped over to her bed and reached under her pillow. She pulled out a utility knife and engaged the blade.

"Interesting," the smaller man said. "I expected a gun."

Her pistol, unfortunately, was still in the truck's glove compartment. She'd never thought she'd need a weapon, but had taken the gun safety course and bought the pistol as insurance. The knife had been her dad's and she'd been sleeping with it ever since he'd gotten sick.

After what seemed like forever, the big man took a forward step. She hadn't wrapped her mind around his size, but at least he no longer shocked her. He simply was what he was, a threat to her existence.

The window. Dive through it while keeping the knife

away from her body. Run no matter what happened to her feet. Run while the damn bastards were trying to decide what to do.

She was still trying to convince herself that she stood a chance of getting away when big man took another step.

"Don't!" She sounded more scared than determined. "Damn you, don't!" She pointed the knife at his throat.

He reached for her. Gasping, she scrambled back.

The way he studied her made her wonder if he was concerned she might cut herself. If he was, did that mean they didn't intend to kill her?

"You're not going to get away." His voice put her in mind of rumbling thunder. "Don't make it any harder than it needs to be."

Were they here to kidnap her? That was crazy. No one would pay more than a few bucks for her return.

"Use the Taser," the other man said. "We aren't here to play games."

The way the big man's nostrils flared told her he didn't like being given orders. All right, she wouldn't make that mistake, which left her with one option — the window.

"I want to see what you're made of," Big Man said. "Do you go down without a fight or…?"

Not caring what he was trying to tell her, she jerked back her free arm. Her elbow struck the screen. The screen sagged but didn't pop out. She hit it again, felt it give way.

Holding the knife out from her body, she spun away from Big Man, leaned over, and started to push off with her feet. Before she could dive out of the window, however, powerful hands grabbed her around the waist and yanked her against a solid body.

She screamed and twisted around, slashing wildly. Something struck her wrist, numbing her hand. The knife fell soundlessly to the carpet. She'd just started to kick out when monster-man lifted her off her feet, carried her over to her bed and threw her face-down on it.

"That's how it's done," he announced. She didn't care

whether he was talking to her or his companion, just that with his splayed hand pressing against the small of her back, she couldn't push herself off the bed. She managed to turn her head toward him but wished she hadn't because now she was staring at his crotch.

"You could have injured the merchandize," the other man grumbled. "That's why the Taser—"

"I know what I'm doing."

"Not in this you don't. Damn it, you're supposed to follow instructions."

"Yeah, right."

The bed dipped as he climbed onto it, still holding her down. He straddled her hips and brushed her hair off her cheek.

"You're all right? Nothing injured."

Did he expect her to answer, maybe thank him for being so considerate? Not in this lifetime. Much as she needed to get out from under him, she knew better than to wear herself out attempting the impossible.

"I don't want you talking to her," the other man said. "Keep her off-balance."

"Oh she's off-balance all right. Trust me on that. Okay, Marina, time for me to get to work."

He knew her name, which meant what, that they'd been following her? If they had they must know she lived alone.

Her arms had been out from her sides and useless because she couldn't reach back enough to attack him. When the pressure against the small of her back let up, she sucked in a deep breath. He locked his fingers around her wrists. Even though she resisted, he easily crossed one wrist over the other behind her.

"This is why I don't want her out of it," he said. "I want her aware of everything that's happening."

The other man grumbled. His clothes appeared more expensive than her captor's. Maybe that meant Little Man was supposed to be in charge, maybe her captor's superior. Any other time she probably would have laughed at the notion of Big Man allowing anyone to order him to do anything.

Just as he had no intention of letting her up until he was ready.

A shadow at the side of the bed caught her attention. She stared at Little Man, hating him with every fiber of her being.

"What do you want?" her captor asked.

Little Man folded his arms across a silk shirt and stared down at her the way a hunter with a fresh kill would. "I wanted to see if she's trying to fight you."

She wanted to, all right. In fact, it still took every bit of self-control she had in her not to.

"Fortunately no, she isn't."

"What do you mean, fortunately?"

"I've tamed horses. It's a lot harder getting through to the ones that fight than those that understand who's in charge."

Her captor had compared her to a bronc? She wondered if Big Man and she might have an understanding of horses in common — if she lived long enough to find out.

"Tray, I don't want to stay here," the other man said.

"Neither do I. Let me get her ready."

Ready for what? The smaller man had called Tray by name because they weren't concerned she could identify them. Was their intention to take her somewhere, rape then kill her?

For the first time since she'd spotted the men, terror threatened to overwhelm her. She didn't want to die! Not at twenty-four. Her stomach knotted, her heart raced and she had to work at not losing bladder control. Early in her racing career, another horse had collided with the one she'd been riding and both animals had fallen. Even as the ground and flailing hooves had closed in on her, she hadn't been as afraid as she was now.

"She's shaking," Tray announced.

"Good." Little Man leaned down until his face was inches from hers. "Wondering what's going to happen to you, are you? Go on. Conjure up every scenario you're capable of. It'll give you something to do, something that'll contribute to your undoing."

What are you saying?

"You're messing with her mind," Tray said as she willed her muscles to stop jerking.

"You're damn right I am. Does that surprise you?"

"No." Tray drew out the word. He closed one oversized hand over her crossed wrists, which left the other free for what? "I'm just taking note of your techniques."

"My techniques are based on successful methodology. We know what works — and we expect new employees to follow protocol."

When Tray didn't respond, Little Man frowned. She didn't know what to make of the relationship between her captors any more than she could make sense of what she'd heard about technique, methodology and protocol. With her nervous system on overdrive, she was hard-pressed to accept that her world had been turned on end.

Above and behind her, Tray changed position. She was afraid he'd rest all his weight on the backs of her thighs. Instead, suddenly her left arm was free. Before she could think what to do, metal touched her right wrist.

"No!" She tried to jerk her arm free then started bucking. Doing something felt good. Maybe useless but better than surrender.

Despite her struggle, Tray easily locked the cuff around her wrist and pulled up on the metal, increasing the strain on her shoulder.

Sweating, barely able to concentrate on breathing, she forced herself to stop fighting. Tray lowered her tethered arm so her hand again rested on her buttocks. Then he took hold of her left wrist, pulled it back, and handcuffed her. He released her and leaned back. Was that his erection against her crack? She imagined him thrusting his arms above his head like a cowboy who had just roped and thrown a steer.

"It's simple." He placed his hands on her shoulders and

lifted her upper body off the bed. "All it takes is a pair of handcuffs and you're under my control."

That and his much larger, stronger body.

And her fear.

He continued pulling up until the strain in her back made her gasp. After holding her like that while she likened herself to a hooked fish, he let go. She fell back onto the bed, smashing her breasts. He didn't have to speak for her to understand his message. He could do whatever he wanted to her and she couldn't do a thing to stop him.

He'd rape her and she'd let him. Get the violation over with. Not let him get off on her resistance.

Unless the instinct for self-preservation made that impossible.

Tray's companion brushed her wet hair away from her face. Instead of leaning close again, he stepped back. His gaze roamed over her, every inch Tray's bulk didn't hide. Even though the smaller man was no longer touching her, she felt as if he was mauling her, invading her private space.

Would she ever have that space back?

His attention settled on her face, and she returned his stare. "Lift her again," he said. "I want to check something."

She thought Tray might object to the command, hoped he would. Instead he vised his fingers over her shoulders and effortlessly hauled her back up. The other man grabbed her T-shirt in front and pulled it up, exposing her hanging breasts. She tried to twist away.

"There isn't much substance to her," Tray said. "Pretty small, are they?"

Instead of immediately answering, the man cupped the breast closest to him and kneaded it. She felt sick.

"Surprisingly," he said, "they aren't. What are they, Marina? C cups?"

Like she'd tell him! Like she'd acknowledge what he was doing!

"Decent knockers," Tray said. "That's good."

"Damn good." Little Man's fingers slid down her breast.

216

Instead of letting it go as she prayed, he caught her nipple between thumb and forefinger and squeezed.

Hissing under her breath, she again tried to twist free. Waves of helplessness washed over her. She'd never felt more alive.

"Hey," Tray said. "I thought you wanted to get out of here."

"I do, but the merchandize is distracting."

Merchandize?

The pain radiating out from her nipple, and now over her breast, distanced her from the incomprehensible word. The horrible thought that she'd been given a hint of her future seized her. She fought to keep from sobbing but couldn't.

Her tormentor's hold on her nipple tightened, forcing her to clench her teeth to keep from crying again. She was losing this battle, couldn't keep her pain to herself. Just then Tray again let go of her shoulders and she hit the mattress. A moment passed before she realized Tray's action had forced Little Man to let go of her.

"What the hell was that?" he grumbled. "I wasn't through teaching her a lesson."

"I'm going to be her trainer, not you."

Trainer? As in sex slave trainer?

Her world blurred as she recalled a snippet of conversation she'd overhead between a couple of local businessmen who wagered heavily on horse races. She'd been coming out of the women's restroom one afternoon when she'd spotted them standing near the men's restroom.

"I'd love to see her with a collar around her neck," one of them had said. "Naked and on her knees before me."

"Yeah," the other had responded. "A well-trained sex slave."

More books from Totally Bound Publishing

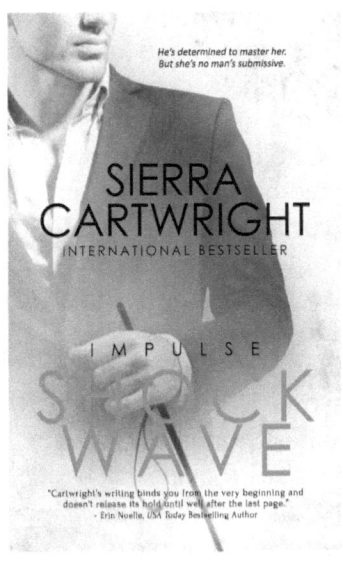

Book one in the Impulse series

There can only be one victor…

Shy and serious by day — insatiable by night.

Sue
Horsford

I felt stronger kneeling at
Gabriel's feet than I ever had
standing at Paul's side

A Fine Line

No one would understand that my submission empowered me, that I felt stronger kneeling at Gabriel's feet than I ever had standing at Paul's side.

She's scared of it – but craves it. He's a pro, but doing it with her scares him too. S & M is scary stuff. For scary, read exciting…

About the Author

Vonna Harper

What prompts a mild-mannered mostly law abiding woman to write erotica and erotic romance, a lot revolving around BDSM and capture/bondage? Is it the complex issue of taking or giving up control?

Vonna Harper doesn't know and she has given up trying to find the answer. It's enough that many readers are drawn to what some call the dark side. All she asks is that readers understand she writes fiction--a brand of fiction she finds fascinating.

Vonna has lost count of the number of books, novellas, and short stories she's written. What she has no doubt of, it's a hell of a ride.

Vonna Harper loves to hear from readers. You can find contact information, website details and an author profile page at https://www.totallybound.com/

TOTALLY
BOUND

Home of Erotic Romance